MW01100856

The Edifice

By

R. K. Holliday

Edited by Flora Brown

Text copyright © 2014 by R.K. Holliday

All rights reserved.

CONTENTS

Shadow

Conner Laurel paced back and forth, confused. He felt exhausted from a very stressful and vivid dream. The night light near his spacecraft shaped bed was still lit and the small bedroom was illuminated dimly. A large shadow of Connor was being cast on the wall. He stared at the shadow for a moment and stretched his arms, legs, and neck. He felt sore. Suddenly there was a soft knock at the door.

"Connor..." a soft and comforting whisper crawled through the door.

"Sweetie?"

The door cracked open, and Connor saw his mother looking half asleep and wearing a dark green robe. She was a slender woman with curly auburn hair barely sweeping her shoulders. Her brown eyes seemed black in the dark as she moved towards Conner and knelt down.

"Why are you awake, dear? Are you frightened?"

"No mom, it was just a dream."

"Another dream? That's the second one this week.... Maybe it's the night light, or perhaps we should eat earlier before bed." She was really speaking to herself trying to sort her thoughts.

"Mom…"

She seemed to stop thinking and asked her son softly, "What dear?"

"In my dream, I was in tall grass. I was wearing my pajamas, but it was cold. The sky was bright with stars. The moon was almost as bright as the sun. I saw someone there. He was an older man I think. It was hard to see. He told me that I needed to go back. That it wasn't my time. I was quite scared, and I began to step back. As I did, I tumbled down a hill, and it really hurt. The man ran to the edge of the hill towards me. I was breathless, but I was more afraid of him than the fall. He shouted at me.... He shouted, but I could barely make it out. I only heard one or two words, but I didn't understand them."

"That is quite an imagination you have, sweetie. Are you afraid? Do you want to sleep with us? "

"No mom… I'll be ok. I'm just confused."

"Well, I'll get you something to drink, and we'll get you right back to bed."

She patted his head softly and left the room to get him a beverage.

Connor turned back to his shadow and put all of his thoughts and focus on trying to remember what the man in the dream said. He felt compelled to know, but he didn't know why. His mother returned to the room with a drink and tucked him back into his sheets.

"Sip on this dear."

He took one sip and said, "Actually, mom, I'm not all that thirsty."

"That's fine dear. All you have to do is call, and I'll bring you something. "

"Thanks," he replied as he rolled over away from the shine of his nightlight.

His mother reached and turned the light off. "This will probably help you sleep, good night, dear." She slowly made her way back towards his doorway in the dark trying not to stumble over anything. Connor with eyes wide open stared into the darkness. It was as if the darkness brought him clarity for a moment. Slowly his eyelids drifted. His lips began to crack open. He was completely exhausted and was on the brink of falling asleep. He softly mumbled, "impetus."

Suddenly, a shattering crash rung through the hallway and into his bedroom. He quickly rolled back over in panic. His mother had dropped the glass she had given him earlier and he could hear her breathing heavily. Connor sensed her scrambling to pick up the pieces of glass....

Before Connor could get up and check on her, she announced, "I'm alright dear... I'm alright...." She gathered the last piece of glass and Connor listened as she eerily crept further down the hall.

The next morning, Connor awoke to the sun shining through his bedroom window. His old airplane mobile reflected light around the room. The planes circling were older models, but it didn't matter. Connor enjoyed the idea of flying. His father would talk about Conner's grandfather and how he was a great pilot in his time. Connor would never know his grandfather, but it fascinated him all the same. He sat up, stretched his legs, and was off to the bathroom. As he walked into the bathroom, he noticed himself in the mirror. Connor had light brown hair that stood tall like broom bristles. He had blue eyes and thin lips.

As he began to brush his teeth, he noticed a dark mark on his hand. He wondered if he had bumped into someone or something yesterday and just didn't notice. He rinsed his mouth and caught the smell of breakfast making its way up the stairs. Since Connor was slender, he always felt like he should eat often. The other kids his age were getting bigger and taller than him. He felt behind from the others in his class. As he walked out of the bathroom and started for the stairs, he felt a tiny sting on the bottom of his foot. The pinch was enough for him to hobble and wince. Connor lifted his foot to check what caused this pain. He didn't notice anything on his foot, and the pain seemed to go away as quickly as a candle being blown out.

"Was it a bug?" He looked around for a moment but didn't notice anything creeping about.

He started down the stairs. Merely four steps down, he stepped on a small piece of glass. He winced again and immediately became stressed. He frantically grabbed the railing to balance and rechecked his foot. This time there was a tiny piece of glass in his foot causing him to bleed lightly. He grabbed the piece of glass with his fingernails and pulled it out. Connor let out a big sigh and remembered his mother dropping the glass last night. He hobbled on down the stairs and grabbed a tissue from the table near the entrance of his house. He leaned on the wall and wiped the blood from his foot. The bleeding seemed to stop.

He looked outside and saw his neighbor scrounging in the mailbox across the street. The house across the street was almost identical compared to his. Connor was in a "tight" area of the town where all of the houses were of similar layouts. It was easy to hear other people's gatherings or their cars pulling out of driveways. In the summers, you could smell a neighbor cooking meat four houses down. The only smell that concerned Connor, however, was the eggs he smelled in the kitchen. He was very hungry after all.

His second sight of the day was his father rummaging through old cabinets in the kitchen. Timothy Laurel was of average build with straight dark hair. His hair shinned with gel and was pushed back by a fine toothed comb. His shirt was buttoned but untucked from his slacks.

"Where does that woman hide the sugar?" He said under his breath as he checked behind every item. There were bacon and eggs slowly cooking on the stove as Connor's stomach growled.

"Good God! Is there a dinosaur in here?!" Timothy said jokingly as he turned and smiled at his son. He had a smirk of achievement as he shook the sugar to show his prize. He opened the top and emptied its contents into a shallow cup of coffee.

"Morning, dad."

"I think you're taller today."

"Pshhh..." Connor squeaked, "I wish...."

"No, really, you're getting bigger every day," as he sipped his hot liquid slowly. "You know, I think you have a birthday coming up!"

"Already?!" A bright voice came from the laundry room. Sybil Laurel, Connor's mother, was wearing the same robe as the night before as she dropped a basket of clothing in the edge of the family room. "Whatever will we do with a teenager in this house?!"

Connor smiled shyly and asked, "Isn't it an off day?"

"For you it is," Timothy replied.

"What about you? You're working today?" Connor asked inquisitively.

"I have to go down to the factory for a meeting. You'll understand one day." Timothy checked his old bronzed time piece and blurted in his drink as he caught sight of the long hand. "Blazes I gotta get a move on... but hey, sport, right quick.... Have you thought about what you want for your birthday?"

"Well, there's a cool exhibit at the Briar's museum where you get to try out planes and ships. There's an ice cream shop nearby as well. I was hoping a few friends could come with us." Connor explained.

"Try out planes?" Timothy looked at Sybil wondering what Connor meant.

"Oh, it's a simulation. I saw it on the TV a couple of days ago," she responded as she grabbed the breakfast off the stove and placed it on plates.

"Oh right, right," Timothy said. "I might be able to show you a thing or two then. Your grandfather used to talk to me for hours about maneuvers and strategies."

"Yeah right," Connor replied.

Timothy kissed each of their heads, placed his cup in the sink, and scurried out of the door. Connor sat down at the tiny kitchen table and started scarfing his food down quickly.

"Slow down, dear!"

"Sorry, mom," he replied.

Sybil steadily cut her meat and eggs before taking a tiny bite.

"Mom, I stepped on a piece of glass from last night."

"What?! Are you alright?! Let me see!" she exclaimed.

"Mom, it's fine, it's not even bleeding anymore, and I got it out…. Did you stumble or something?"

She seemed to get a light glaze over her eyes as she stared out through the tiny kitchen window. "No... no... I've just been a little off lately."

Connor quickly took his last bite of food and drank a large portion of his milk in one gulp.

"Mom, what's impetus?"

Sybil slammed her fork on the table loudly. It startled Connor as he stared at her, perplexed. "Where did you hear that? Did you read it?!"

"No."

"Did one of your little friends as school mention it?!" she continued to raise her voice.

"No, mom, I don't --"

"Don't lie to me, Connor Laurel! Are you toying with me?!"

"Mom, no I swear! What's wrong?" he replied in a panic.

She stood quickly and dashed into the family room. He looked through the front window that faced their street. Sybil quickly examined the street to the left and right and closed the curtains quickly.

"Sit down!" she exclaimed pointing to the couch.

"Why? What is going on---?"

"Sit!!! Down!!!" She stopped in her tracks and pointed again at the couch.

He sat down in hopes that she'd calm down. She had never acted this way before on an average *off* day. He felt that something must be terribly wrong. He looked down at his feet as he sat and noticed dirt marks on his left foot that matched the marks on his hand. Connor also still felt a faint sting on the bottom of his foot from stepping on glass.

Sybil marched into the hallway. Connor could hear her frantically digging through a closet. He suddenly became tense that she may be searching for his father's old gun. She hurried back into the room and held a blue pamphlet in front of his face.

"Have you seen this?!"

"What?" he was more confused than before.

"So help me, Connor! Have you been snooping?! And did you find this?!"

"No, mom, I swear I've never seen it before. What is it?"

She fell down on the ground and a tear started down her cheek. She sat there with her head down and her palm open as the pamphlet fell to the ground beside her. Connor looked down at his mother in this submissive form and struggled to understand. This reminded him last night's dream. He knew he would wake up at any moment and would see his shadow casting on his small bedroom wall. But he didn't wake up. He looked around the room and then he fixed his eyes on the open pamphlet. Connor squinted his eyes to see if he could make out a word. He was too frightened to move because his mother was still there whimpering and staring at the ground.

His eyes locked on a dim word in a bold font and with chills, he said the word softly... "Impetus."

Balloon

Connor sat at the kitchen table holding the pamphlet in his hands. The bottom right had a number to call scrolling in a marque across the pamphlet. It was not only paper but an electronic display device as well. The technology was common on important documents. Connor's report cards had always displayed messages for his parents from his headmaster and teachers.

"I didn't tell you or your father because I didn't want either of you to worry. Everyone has been so cheerful and your birthday is coming up." Sybil's eyes were still wet from weeping. She slowly sipped on coffee as she looked at her precious son. She hoped that it was all nothing, but she had a bad feeling.

The pamphlet read:

Attention: This is a public notice from the United Eden Federation (U.E.F.) Our systems have been alerted that there could be a virus in your community. This virus can be very dangerous. It is most commonly found in children. We will continue to scan the area to make sure you and your family are completely safe. The Impetus virus is not contagious if it is contained in a timely manner. If you or someone you know has the following symptoms, please contact us immediately:

Insomnia

Fatigue

Uncommon behavior

Increase in complaints

Confusion

Restlessness

Aggression

Hallucinations

Contact us at 9-080-23472

This message has been approved by the Greater Coalition

"Mom, who is the U.E.F.?" Connor asked his mother.

"I have no idea, sweetie. I asked Samantha Baker's mother if she knew. She received the pamphlet the same day."

"Is Samantha's mom ok? Is she sick?" Connor asked nervously.

"She's fine sweetie. Her mother said she isn't showing any of the symptoms."

"Am I sick?" Connor inquired as he folded the pamphlet up and placed it on the table.

"I really don't think so, sweetie. I don't think you have any of these symptoms…" she sniffled. "Go to your room dear. I'm going to call your father."

Without replying, Connor made his way up the stairs. He went into the bathroom before going to his room. He gazed into the mirror and attempted to hold in his tears. He had never been so scared in his life. He was clueless and desperate. The thought of his mother being so distraught brought water to his eye. Connor wiped away his tear, and as he did, he saw the mark on his hand in the mirror again. As he focused on the mark of dirt, he felt a gradual sensation of heat on his skin. It scared him. He started to breathe heavily and sat down on the cool floor. He sat on the ground for a minute or two. Suddenly the heat radiating through his skin vanished.

"What's happening to me?" he murmured under his breath. He shook his head and tried to lose the sense of fear within his mind. Connor placed his hands on the bathroom wall and bravely stood back up. He suddenly felt normal again.

I might as well get clean, he thought to himself. He took off his pajamas and discovered more dirt than he had seen earlier that morning. He stepped into the tub and embraced the warm shower.

Hours passed, and Connor remained in his room. He took out his headset and began playing his favorite game. The headset was a typical device used for information searches and other purposes. Most of the applications programmed into his headset were games and various books. Connor found solace in playing a piloting game from time to time. As he played, he was astonished that he had beaten his high score. He started to lose focus on the game and became worried about his mother. He heard the door open swiftly downstairs.

"How is he?! What's going on?!" his father's voice echoed up the stairs.

"Here! Here! This is it," his mother replied. Their voices began to fade as they moved around the house.

"Now just calm down. Let me try to wrap my head around this," his father's voice faded.

Connor slowly crept down the stairs to greet his father as softly as possible. His mother and father were discussing the situation as Connor entered the kitchen.

"Hi, dad."

Each of his parents froze and looked over at him.

"Hey, kiddo, how are you feeling?" his dad asked trying to smooth the mood.

"I feel fine. Can I go out back? I haven't been out all day," he asked expecting a sharp denial.

"Uh, sure son, go ahead... just let us know if you need anything. We'll be right here."

Connor walked outside to his tiny backyard. His backyard was connected to a couple of other small backyards by short brick fences. There was hardly any privacy in his town, but he felt safe there. He started to kick around his ball he left outside. He swiftly kicked the dirty ball at a chipped brick on the back side of his fence. He would, from time to time, aim at the chip in the wall. Connor used this as a target since he didn't have enough room for a proper net or goal. He noticed an object in the neighboring house directly behind the wall. He could hardly make it out and always felt like a peeping Tom straining to see inside other people's windows. From an early age, his mother would remind him not to look through anyone's windows if they were open. She claimed it was rude.

He kicked the ball forcefully. As it hit the chipped brick, the neighbor's back door flew open. A petite blonde girl pranced out into the yard holding a bobbly orange balloon in hand. She had freckles and dark eyebrows. She seemed to be always smiling when Connor saw her. It was his neighbor Samantha Baker.

"Hi, Connor, why so gloomy?!" she shouted.

Startled by the greeting, he quickly forced a smile and replied, "What do you mean, Sam?"

"You look down, oh well... do you like my balloon?!" she spun around in a circle as she pranced toward the fence.

"Um, yeh, it's very nice... where did you get it?" he asked as upbeat as he could.

"'There was a clown selling them at the grocery and mom let me get one! It reminds me of the sun!" she leaned on the brick fence with her back facing Connor. He was two years older than her. However, he didn't ignore her. Connor always tried to talk to her at school. He knew that the conversations would be short since she was always oozing energy. Though, she always made him feel accepted.

She looked up at the balloon bouncing against the blue sky background, and Connor's eyes caught the same view. "You know, Connor… I'm almost as tall as you are now!" she chuckled. Samantha ran back into her house with the balloon chasing behind. It bounced and bobbled as if it were attempting to beat every surface it could find.

"Maybe so, Sam…" he spoke softly as she slammed the door behind her.

"Connor! Come on in, son!" his father yelled at him through the kitchen window.

Rain

As time passed by, there were still tensions in the Laurel home. Every other day Sybil would weep, and Connor felt responsible. Unfortunately, he had no idea how to make the situation better. He spent more time in his room than usual. He thought maybe staying out of sight may decrease his mother's fits. For the first time in his life, he felt like his father was lucky to be away at the factory for long hours during *On* days.

Two weeks from my birthday... Connor thought to himself as he browsed the calendar on his headset. An alert showed that a storm could hit his area as he viewed the dates. He heard a faint jingle outside his window and in the distance. He took off his headset and walked to his window to examine the back yard. He first noticed the dark clouds slowly sailing his way as they slithered over the edge of the sun.

"Connor!"

A high pitched greeting caught his attention. It was Samantha with a new bike, but she barely had enough room to ride in her backyard. She waved and clicked her bell to make a jingle. Connor simply waved back and smiled. She pulled her bike to the edge of her house and leaned it against the wall. She held out her hand and looked up. It looked like rain and in her case felt like it too.

"I should probably invite her to the museum on my birthday," he said to himself regrettably. He imagined her breaking something in the exhibit and his entire party being escorted from the premises.

"Maybe not..." he chuckled.

He sat back down on his bed and put on his headset.

"Draken," he said clearly. His headset brought up an outline of a media player. "Play," he commanded.

A cartoon called *Draken* began playing an episode within the headset. *Draken* was one of his favorite shows. It featured a boy a few years older than himself who could turn into a dragon. However, he didn't always turn into a dragon in the show unless it was absolutely necessary. He usually completed tasks in the shape of a boy who had extremely tough skin and a fire-breathing mouth. His mouth could also be incredibly witty. Not only was he stronger than every foe but smarter. He spent day after day helping others in need and never asked for restitution. He faced terrible horrors, but he never lost a fight so far as Connor had noticed. He continued to watch. It was common for Draken's challenges to become harder as each episode ended.

"Draken always figures out what's going on before the others," Connor thought to himself as the dialog played along. *I want to be as good as Draken.*

A while later, his father arrived home. He came in the doorway and hung his dry coat on the rack as he had just missed the rain. Connor hurried downstairs to greet his father.

"Hi, sport," his dad rubbed his head and looked towards the kitchen.

"You're home early, Tim," his mother announced.

"The boss let us go so we could beat the storm."

"Oh, you know... we really should get Mr. Riley a gift for his birthday or anniversary this year," Sybil suggested.

"Well, he's not really a gift man. I've never seen the others give him anything," he replied. "Plus, the only gift giving that needs to happen is in two weeks for this kid," he said through the side of his mouth as he nodded at Connor. Connor smiled proudly.

"Well it was just a thought, dear," Sybil murmured as she turned back into the kitchen.

"What's on the TV, sport?" his dad asked playfully as he announced. "TV.... On...."

The display quickly grew in size and projected an image. Connor and his dad walked to the couch and sat down for a moment. A commercial played with an overly excited man shouting grand promises for a safer and less expensive future.

"COME TRY ONE OUR NEW HOVE ROVERS! IT'S RATED THE SAFEST IN ITS CLASS AND IT'S GREAT FOR THE ENVIRONMENT. FLY TO WORK A FEW MINUTES QUICKER WHILE SHOWING UP OTHERS WITH OUR NEW CHROME EXTERIOR."

The salesman continued to ramble for what seemed like an eternity.

"Dad, when are we going to get a flying car?"

"Oh rubbish! The roads are just fine Connor! They've hardly regulated that flying car stuff anyways. I read that there's a crash every day with those things," Timothy spouted.

"NOW WITH IMPROVED LANDING MECHANISMS YOU CAN FEEL SAFER AS YOU TAKE THE KIDS TO SCHOOL OR THE BIG GAME!!!" The salesman continued to shout through the ad.

"Well, he says they're safe," Connor shrugged.

"Well, even if that is the case. If we get one of those, you don't get to go to your exhibit and ice cream shop. In fact, we may have to sell you all together!" his father joked.

"Oh come on!" Connor played along.

"Honey, can you help me with this?" Sybil's voice echoed through the house.

Timothy jumped up quickly and ran into the kitchen. At that moment, Connor heard a rumble not far in the distance down the street. As the salesman kept on blabbering in the background, Connor walked towards the window that overlooked the front street. He noticed an unusually large car slowing down and stopping two houses down. The car was black and bulbous and the windows matched. Connor had never seen a car like this. Two men got out at the same time. The one from the driver's side was dark skinned, tall, and stood as straight as an arrow. He wore a black trench coat with ceremonial blue military clothing underneath. He was bald and seemed quite down to business. He stepped around the vehicle towards a house opposite of Connor's. From the passenger side of the car arose another man with parted hair and a trimmed beard. He also wore a trench coat but had gray robes underneath. He seemed concerned as he examined his surroundings. As the men passed by one another, they each looked at each other seemingly saying nothing and then looked towards the sky. At that moment, the rain started to fall in a harsh shower. They looked at each other again and moved on to the neighbors' door.

"Mum... dad... who are those men?" he said loudly enough for them to hear.

Sybil came to the window to see what Connor was asking about. As she caught a glimpse of them, the dark skinned man was speaking to the neighbor and showing him a tablet. The neighbor shook his head and pointed towards Connor's house. Sybil quickly closed the curtains.

"Connor... go upstairs. Wait in your room," she said sourly.

"Ok..." Connor agreed and started up the stairs. The last thing he wanted was for his mother to weep or get scared again. Before he got to his room, he felt a moment of bravery or perhaps defiance as he put his back to the wall in the stairway so that he could listen to the events unfold.

"Did you call them?!" Sybil shouted.

"No, we agreed that everything was fine! I would never keep that from you," Connor's father answered with a stern tone.

The house suddenly turned as cold as icicles, leaving the familiar warmth a short memory. A knock at the door echoed through the house. Everyone in the house hesitated to move, and Connor held his breath. After a moment, a harder knock rang out with a shocking announcement.

"U.E.F., please open the door. We would like to have a word with you!" a man shouted in a neutral tone.

Timothy started towards the door as Sybil grabbed the back of his shirt to stop him softly in his tracks. She looked him in the eye, then looked at the ground, and eased her hands off her husband's shirt.

Another round of knocks barraged the door. "Please, this is urgent business! We've been approved by the Coalition to speak with you."

Connor slowly slipped further out of sight as best he could without losing a view from the scene. Connor's father opened the door to a drenched man and his colleague standing close behind.

"May we come in, sir?" the second man asked graciously behind the decorated gentleman.

As Timothy was about to allow them in from the wet exterior, Sybil jumped beside him.

"Wait, what's this about? You can't expect us to just let anyone into our home without any reason or identification," she explained.

The second man opened his coat and showed a badge that gleamed with government authenticity.

The dark man in front began to speak, "I'm sure you're aware that there is a rare virus that has been discovered in this area. It's our job to contain that virus and eliminate the threat and possible harm to others."

The second man placed a hand on the military man's shoulder and stepped a bit more forward.

"What my friend is trying to say here is that we think that someone could be terribly ill and we want to make sure they get treatment without harming others in the area. Please do forgive him… he's been in the military his entire life," the second man calmly replied stepping closer to the door.

"Why is military involved?" Timothy scoffed.

"Well, kind sir, it is a matter of national security. Oh, and I'm sorry we didn't announce this earlier but I'm Dr. Ferdinand Finn, and this is Colonel Albert."

"Fifth Battalion," the colonel murmured.

"Quite right, the fifth battalion… Pardon my manners Colonel," Dr. Finn went on graciously.

"No harm will come to anyone here I assure you, sir and madam. Our systems have given us an outline of who may be carrying the *Impetus* virus," Dr. Finn explained as he signaled the colonel to show the tablet.

Completely puzzled Timothy and Sybil looked on to a display of a three-dimensional model of their son. It was almost an exact match. There were only vague details of his facial structure that seemed a bit off, but there was no denying it was him. Dr. Finn caught a glimpse upstairs from out of the doorway and nudged the colonel as he continued to stare. The colonel slowly lowered the display as a figure caught his attention. Timothy and Sybil realizing these men were no longer in the conversation each turned around to see Connor standing boldly at the top of the stairs stunned by what he had just heard and witnessed.

<u>Manual</u>

Connor leaned back far on the couch so that he could stretch his legs. He'd been sitting there for a while as the conversation in the kitchen played out.

"Now this seems very horrible, and it possibly is, but I assure you we are very good at what we do," Dr. Finn explained. He was sitting at the kitchen table sipping coffee that Sybil had made fresh for him and his companion. The Colonel was sitting across the table from Dr. Finn taking notes on this tablet. Timothy looked at his wife as they stood near the kitchen window while leaning on the counters. Rain continued to fall rapidly and tap the glass behind them.

"What exactly do we need to do? He's just a boy, and we're all very tense about this," Timothy spoke up.

"How did you get that image of our son? Have you spied on us?" Sybil blurted out.

"No, no, you see we have a very advanced system that scans the globe looking for people, namely children who may have this problem. Once it pinpoints an area, we start looking.

Over time, as the virus grows our system can begin putting together a genetic make-up of the host. It's very advanced stuff, but it has to be. We're trying to protect people," Dr. Finn went on. "The earlier we find the child, the better chance the child has of making a full recovery, and we lower the risk of the virus spreading. You shouldn't worry though... it takes a while for the virus to develop fully. Nevertheless, we always want to be precautious."

"You should have called us," the Colonel said stiffly as he looked at the pamphlet on the table. He didn't miss a beat as he kept working.

"Oh.... Well, we're very sorry!" Sybil said sarcastically. "We can't read our son's genetic code as easily as an *advanced system*."

Colonel Albert didn't react, he just kept reading and logging.

"So what's the process? What do we do?" Timothy asked with some reserve.

"The boy... will have to come with us," Dr. Finn replied.

"Well, we can all go together. I can call Mr. Riley and make sure I get a few days off," he nodded towards Sybil.

"I'm afraid… actually… that the boy will have to come with us for several months..." Dr. Finn added.

"Absolutely out of the question!" Timothy fretted.

"He has school! And it's not good for a boy to be alone! I can visit most days, but I can't live at a med center!" Sybil concluded.

"Please, please do calm down. First, this facility is one of the most advanced facilities on the planet. The boy will have access to learning materials and even a classroom setting while he's there. Everything we offer is top notch. It's just as much accommodating as a top rate hotel I assure you. Secondly, there is more than just he who has this virus. There are several hundred children all over the world that have developed this problem. He will surely not be alone. My daughter is there now...."

He said with a soft throat.

"Oh, that's.... That's awful," Sybil responded with her hand covering her mouth.

"It's fine. It's fine. Finally, you won't be able to come along. It's very dangerous to allow outsiders into the area because we aren't entirely sure who else could carry it. Sure, you most likely don't have it yet from what our intelligence describes, but we don't want to risk you contacting hundreds of other carriers. You can speak to him from time to time though via live comm links. For the first month which is undoubtedly the hardest, there will be no communications. Your son will spend most of that time in testing and being scanned," Dr. Finn informed.

"When can we have him back here?" Sybil inquired.

"Judging by the average time he could be home in April or maybe as late as May." Dr. Finn continued, "If we can scan him properly, he could visit home for a short stay. However, he would be monitored while away from the facility. There are strict guidelines to that process. That hardly happens I'm sorry to say… collecting data can take time."

Sybil gasped, and her jaw dropped as though it was magnetized to the floor.

"Will he suffer? Will it be painful?" Timothy whimpered.

Dr. Finn pushed his coffee away a bit and stood up from the table. He walked over to Timothy who had his head hanging low like a willow tree without a breeze.

"Now see, Tim... that is the good news. When we catch it early like this, we don't have to do much but monitor it. There's a chance that the virus will be fought off by his body after a while. We never give them medication or invasive treatments at first because we don't want to aggravate the virus and cause it to multiply. In short, we hope that he's like most cases and he fights it off alone. I won't be dishonest, though. This can grow to be a very dangerous and unjust occasion, but we have gotten very good at keeping that at bay," Dr. Finn consoled. "I promise both of you that I will look after him and care for him just as I have my own daughter," he vowed as he made eye contact with each of them.

The Colonel placed his tablet on the table as a display of a tiny man popped out and hovered above. He stepped forward and announced:

"I am very sorry that this misfortune has come to your home. My office and I vow to take every possible measure to ensure that your loved one is safe, secure, and treated with the utmost care. This problem concerns us and many others, and we will fight to bring your loved one back home to you as soon as possible. Our prayers, our thoughts, and our steadfast hope go out to you at this time. These officers will escort your loved one to a

safe and stable area where life will go on as normally as possible. Please help us preserve all that we love by cooperating with them in this difficult time. We thank you for being brave…."

Underneath the man, a fine signature is projected that reads:

"Premier Douglas Icarus"

"My god… that was the Premier of the Greater Coalition," Sybil wept. She felt for the first time a deep sinking feeling in her stomach. This was real and it was happening whether she was ready for it or not.

Colonel Albert grabbed his tablet, stood up straight, and turned almost mechanically towards the three of them.

"We'll be sending you a sum of assistance money to your account to help you in this time… I'll be in the car," he directed as he walked towards the door. He grabbed his wet coat off the rack, and as he put it on, he stared at Connor intently. Connor with a straight face stared back. The Colonel cracked a half sided smile, opened the door, and walked out closing the door behind him.

As he was leaving, Timothy looked at Dr. Finn and growled, "You can't just buy my boy."

"I assure you we aren't buying anyone. It is a system set in place to help families in this time. That's all. It's not a lot, but it will help with food and other necessities," he assured them.

He turned towards the living room and said as he walked, "We would like to be going now. We'll be back at 7:00 am tomorrow morning for the boy. He won't need to bring anything extra. He can pack only items of sentiment if he so chooses. We'll provide clothing, food, and cater to all of his needs." He put on his coat waved to Timothy and Sybil and gave a quick nod and smile to Connor who was still sitting on the couch.

He walked out, and they all listened as the car drove away.

Sybil and Timothy walked into the family room to find Connor sitting on the couch with a puzzled look in his eye.

"Well-" Timothy started to speak with his son.

"I guess we won't be going anywhere for my birthday then..." Connor interjected.

Timothy's heart grew sad, but he forced out a joyful demeanor the best he could. He knelt down and put his hand on Connor's knee. "I guess not, Sport... I guess not..." he choked.

Sybil stood there watching and wishing that time could stand still forever. But she could only muster a single action, "I'm going to make some dinner. How about some potatoes how you like them, dear?" she proposed.

Connor looked up to his mother and simply shook his head yes.

She walked into the kitchen to start cooking. Timothy sat down beside his son and put his arm around him as fathers do and gave him a stiff hug.

They sat on the couch and simply looked through the window until dinner was ready.

The family ate and spoke in a normal fashion. It was special to them, and in their own way, it was a temporary goodbye to a life they each loved.

Early the next morning, Connor woke up with a soft headache. It was an ache enough to wake him just as the sun rose and a beam of light hit his window. He touched his head, and the pain left him as he sat up. He went to the window to view the sunrise, and as he opened his curtains wide, he saw Samantha's bike turned over in her yard.

It must have fallen over last night during the rain, he thought to himself. There didn't seem to be any major damage but all the same, this reminded him that he wouldn't be seeing Samantha for quite a while. "Who will she bug now?" he chuckled as he enjoyed the morning view. I better write her a letter explaining what's going on. Connor went over to his headset to record a message but realized that she probably didn't have a headset yet. *I didn't get mine until last year actually*, he pondered. He then went into his tiny closet to rummage around for any kind of paper and pen.

I think I have something... somewhere.... he thought. Connor opened his closet. He rummaged through old clothes and toys from his younger years. He then looked up in the top of the closet and saw a box. "Hmmm...."

He stood on his tip toes to try to reach the box but could barely touch the bottom of it. The edge was just a bit off the shelf, and he tried to shimmy it towards him. He hobbled and leaped a few times and with luck moved the box closer and closer to the edge. *Almost... there,* he thought as he took a last big leap to knock it down. He miscalculated while in the air and rattled the shelf forcing the box to come falling quicker than he anticipated. Before he could react, the box hit him on the temple and fell open on the floor emptying its contents.

Connor took a deep breath of relief that the task was over and rubbed his head a bit. He noticed that colorful markers and some paper had fallen out of the box. A picture of him from his first year of school was also in the box. He laughed at himself because he was missing some teeth and looked quite dumb in his pink shirt. "Oh, mom... why?" he smiled. He found a green marker that hadn't dried out and a small notepad that had a few empty pages. Most of the pages were full of his senseless drawings from years past. He wrote:

Dear Sam, I will be going away to a new place this year. It's kind of like a center for children. I hope to be back by next spring. The new school year is about to start, and I think you'll love Mrs. Penelope. She has been my favorite instructor so far.

Connor

P.S. I like your bike!

It felt harsh to him that he would be gone. He never desired to go to a new place and especially not to a medical center. He hoped to fit in at least. He felt that surely he would at least be the same height as everyone else.

If everyone is there for the same reason, then surely we will all get along. Maybe I'll be the tallest one there, he thought to himself. He was hopeful and brave even though he didn't know what to expect. Connor washed up and changed out of his pajamas and into a red shirt with brown pants. He wore these clothes often. The colors reminded him of the clothes that Draken wore on the TV show. He grabbed the letter for Sam, stepped downstairs, and entered the kitchen. His mother and father had made him a huge breakfast! There were a couple of balloons and even a homemade cake. However, Timothy and Sybil were not in the kitchen.

Connor smiled and jumped towards the cake. He thought for a moment if he should try some icing. He briefly looked over each shoulder and dug a finger into the edge. "Mmmmm... Strawberry!" The back door opened wide.

"Happy birthday!" Sybil, Timothy, and even Sam shouted.

"It's not my birthday yet," he smiled and continued, "what are you doing here, Sam?!"

He shoved the letter into his pocket.

"I'm here for cake!" she shouted trying to imitate a robot. "I've never had cake for breakfast, Connor. Have you?" she asked.

"No, no, never," he snickered.

"We know it's not your birthday yet, but we wanted to celebrate since we may not be with you on your real birthday," Timothy said with positivity.

"My boy is almost a man!" Sybil said as she put her hands on each of his cheeks and gave him a kiss. Samantha giggled at the sight. Sybil went on to light 13 candles for Connor, and he blew them out swiftly. They ate cake and talked for a while.

"We saw Samantha outside, and we asked her mom if she could join us," Sybil explained.

"Mmmhmmm... she said yes," Samantha agreed as she licked icing from her spoon.

"We would have invited more of your little friends, but I doubt any of them are awake," Timothy mentioned in a lighthearted manner.

"Whelp! I'm done! Thanks for the cake Mrs. Sybil and happy birthday, Connor!" she yelled. She sat her bowl down, gave Connor a big hug, and ran through the back door as fast as a rabbit.

"Oh..." Connor thought to himself as he felt the stiff paper in his pocket. He pulled it out and presented it to his mother. "Mom, will you give this to Samantha when she slows down a bit? I didn't know if I'd see her before I had to go," he stuttered.

"Why yes, dear, I will. You're such a sweet boy," she toyed.

"Mom..." he moaned as he rolled his eyes. He looked up at his father who had a big grin on his face.

"What a heartbreaker!" Timothy joked.

"Get outta here, dad!" he smiled as he was lightly annoyed.

Timothy chuckled a bit and sat his fork onto the table. "Oh, son, listen. You're going to be 13 this year. I wanted to give you something since you're a man now."

"Dad...."

"No, listen, I'm serious, this means a lot to me," he explained as he handed him a poorly wrapped object in old brown paper bags.

Sybil placed a few plates in the sink as she commented, "No time to find proper wrapping, sweetie."

Connor opened the wrapping and was overwhelmed by an old smell. He cleared the wrapping away completely and turned a book around upright so he could read it properly. It was faded white with blue writing on the front. There were tiny brown marks around the binding that suggested it may have gotten wet in the past. He placed his hand on the book. It felt as rough as leather. Connor wasn't sure if it would fall apart if he flipped through the pages.

"Aerial Tactics and Strategies?" he read slowly. Somewhat perplexed, he asked, "What is it? I mean, I know it's a book but what's it about?"

"Well, son, I've had that for a while now. That was your grandfather's flight manual. It's authentic, and it's in ok shape. There are a couple of splotches and tears in the paper, but it's been in our family for a long time. I want you to have it. I trust you with it." Timothy went on, "Some of it you may not understand... there's a lot that I don't understand myself, but there's a few notes written in that help. I think you'll like it."

"Dad, I can't take this... this is special," Connor remarked.

"You're special," Sybil replied.

"She's right, son. Happy birthday," he confirmed.

"Wow thanks, dad! I'll keep great care of this I promise. I won't let anyone lay an eye on it! No one will ever touch it but me!" Connor said convincingly.

"It's fine, we know. We know you'll treat it well," Timothy replied.

The moment seemed surreal to Connor. He was excited and very happy. He knew that the manual wasn't a test or challenge. It was their way of telling Connor that they trusted him to be good and well while he was away from them.

Knock, knock. Knock! Knock! Knock! Was the sound that came from the front door. There was no second guessing who was on the other side. It was 7:00 am, and Connor was about to go it alone. Sybil walked towards the door as it felt like her feet were made of heavy bricks. She did not want to answer the door. She did not want the morning to end.

Dr. Finn was at the door as it opened and he was dressed in the same clothing as yesterday, but it didn't seem worn or dirty. "Good morning, folks. May I?" he signaled to come inside.

"Yes, yes," Sybil answered.

"Where's the Colonel?" Timothy asked as he and Connor walked toward the front door from the kitchen.

"Keeping the engine warm, I'm afraid. I would like to be quite quick you see. We are a bit behind schedule," he spoke calmly.

He caught a glimpse of Connor holding the old book and asked, "Is that all you'll be bringing then?"

"Um, mom, can I take my night light?" he asked politely.

"Of course, dear," she said.

"Ok, I'll be right back."

Connor scurried up the stairs and walked into his room. He closed the curtains and cleaned up the mess from the box incident. He placed the box on his bed, and he grabbed the night light from his nightstand. He was about to walk out of his bedroom, but suddenly he sat on his bed. He looked around, and tears started falling from his eyes. He was scared. He was about to be taken away for a long time. And not to mention two strangers were taking him to a place he had never been. He was afraid because he just didn't know.

Ten minutes passed, and Dr. Finn looked at his wrist display. "Oh my, I can imagine the Colonel sneering right about now," he chuckled.

Sybil and Timothy were pleasant, but they couldn't laugh at the current state of this event.

"May I go talk to him?" he asked graciously.

"Um... I'm not…" Sybil began.

"Sure," Timothy said sharply interrupting her. "We can trust him now. We'll have to for next few months as it is."

He bowed and thanked Timothy for understanding. He slowly walked up the stairs and noticed Connor's door open. "May I come in?" he inquired.

"Yes," Connor said as he dried his tears quickly.

Dr. Finn walked slowly around the room and slightly examined it. The aircraft mobile caught his eye.

"Now this... this is vintage," he said as he brushed his hand carefully on the models to get a closer look. "Wow... A k-13 Rex. These changed everything." As he examined the model closely, the tip of the wing fell off and bounced on the floor. "I'm terribly sorry, I should have been more careful," he apologized humbly.

"It's ok," Connor replied. "I've had to glue that piece back on several times. My grandfather was A k-13 pilot."

"That is rare. There weren't many of them. I've read about it briefly of course. And um... I'd imagine he gave you that manual." He pointed to the old book Connor was clasping.

"I never knew my grandfather but, I just got this from my dad. He gave it to me for my birthday. He trusts me with it," Connor murmured as he tried to hold back tears.

"That is a big responsibility, Connor. Why don't we walk downstairs and say goodbye to your mom and dad. I'd like to hear more about your grandfather when we get to the car." Dr. Finn consoled Connor and tried to edge him along.

"Promise me..." Connor whispered.

"What? What did you say, Connor?" he inquired as he only heard a mumble.

"Promise me, that you won't take this book or night light. Promise you won't let anything happen to them," he stated as he formed tears again.

"Oh, dear boy... I vow to you that neither of those precious items will be harmed." He bent down to get in closer to Connor. "You're going to a very happy and wonderful place I assure you. You'll see as soon as we leave," he said in a fatherly tone.

Connor felt relieved. In a way, he trusted this stranger for the first time.

"My daughter was just like you. She didn't want to believe me either," he said as he started back down the stairs.

Connor bravely stood up and walked down the stairs. He hugged and kissed each of his parents, and they were very sad. Sybil barely let him loose at all. He promised to be good and to treat the other kids well. His father made him promise not to break any more girls' hearts. Connor snickered and smiled and soaked up the moment to give his father the satisfaction. He started outside with Dr. Finn and waved to his parents as he entered the back door of the biggest car he'd ever seen.

Impetus

Dr. Finn got into the car on the opposite side and spoke into his wrist display. The wrist display wrapped tightly around his arm. "We're ready, Colonel," the car rumbled and began to move. Connor looked back through the tinted window to watch his parents disappear in the distance. It wasn't until they left his view that he took in his surroundings. The car's interior was seemingly as big as his bedroom. It was all black. He had leg room enough for a 7-foot man, and the ceiling was so tall he couldn't touch it if reached. The car stretched far ahead like a limousine or a transport truck.

Dr. Finn asked, "Are you thirsty, Connor?"

"Yes."

"How about water or juice?"

"Water is fine, sir," Connor replied.

Dr. Finn pressed a button on his side console near his arm, and a tray lowered with glistening water in a simple round glass.

"There you are," he said as he pointed to the tray.

Connor reached up and grabbed the glass of water. He started sipping on it. It was quite refreshing.

"Am I going to die?" Connor asked.

"Heavens no! I guess I should explain..." Dr. Finn said as he stretched his neck.

"You see, Connor. You're special. One in a million really. Well, even more than a million. The truth is that your health is perfectly fine. *Impetus...* as it's called, isn't a virus at all. Well, I suppose it could be…. We honestly don't know. That's what we have to tell common folk though."

"Common folk, sir?" he asked.

"Why yes, people who don't have Impetus."

"So you lied to me? You lied to my parents?" Connor frantically questioned.

"Well, not entirely. The truth is that Impetus has never killed someone who has it. At least not that we have recorded. Now, when someone has Impetus but hangs around other regular people, it can get dangerous."

"But sir, this doesn't make any sense. What is it then?" he begged to know.

"Impetus means that you have abilities, Connor. Ones that none of your friends have, ones your parents don't have. No one else has your abilities in most cases. It's not entirely human. It's more than what an ordinary human can do," he said confidently.

"I think you may have the wrong person, doctor. I don't have any abilities. I'm just normal," Connor said as he continued to worry.

"Now, now think about it, Connor. Haven't you ever done anything that no one else has done?" Dr. Finn inquired.

"Um..." Connor thought as hard as he could. He always wanted to be special among his peers after all. He kept pondering for a moment but couldn't come up with anything. "No, sir, I don't know of anything."

"Well let me give you an example, and maybe that'll help you along. I know a boy who can control liquids. He's a bit older than you, but he can make a beautiful fountain display if he likes. Oh and one girl merely a year older than you can change her skin to match her environment."

"Like a lizard?" Connor asked.

"Precisely! Like a lizard! Now imagine, Connor.... If those two I just mentioned were still going through life like normal. You know, among normal people but never learned to control themselves or say… they used their Impetus all the time. Even if they didn't do any harm, people would get very nervous around people like us. We've actually lost people to that. So you see, Connor. We're not only protecting your friends and family, we're protecting you," Dr. Finn explained.

Connor sat in silence watching traffic go by past his window. He started to get quite frustrated. He felt as if he had been cheated and that Dr. Finn was lying. At this point who knows what this crazy man would do to him.

"You're lying! I don't believe you. I mean, I can't do anything! This isn't a cartoon or a fairy tale. What's really going on here?!" he shouted. Connor felt hopeless and wanted to throw his glass of water as hard as he could out of the window or on the floor. He took a deep breath and slammed the water on the tray. As he did so, the tray automatically drove itself back into the ceiling.

Dr. Finn saw that Connor was distraught and held up his wrist display close to his mouth, "Pull over, Colonel."

The car slowed down and pulled to the side of the road. Connor was gazing through the window trying to avoid contact with Dr. Finn. He started to get upset, and a tear fell from his eye. *Great, I'm crying again...* Connor thought. He began sniffling.

Dr. Finn kept looking forward and kept his posture. "You know, Connor. This is all hard to take in. So many people with Impetus have acted the same as you are right now. And they should, it's not fair after all. You didn't choose this. It just happens. Just do me one favor. One favor, and then I'll take you back home if you would like."

"You... you're serious?" he started to dry his tears and gain composure.

Dr. Finn continued to look forward. "Yes, I promise."

"Ok, sir," he agreed.

"Loosen your grip and hold out your left hand," Dr. Finn instructed.

Connor was perplexed but slowly relaxed his fist and turned his hand upward. He held his hand open for a moment and instantly before his eyes he saw colors and mass glow slightly over his hand. He gasped and held his hand open wider. The glow went away and a new model of A K-13 Rex aircraft formed in his hand. It was just like the one from his bedroom except brand new.

"But... but... how?" he stuttered nervously and looked at Dr. Finn.

Dr. Finn glanced slowly and made eye contact with Connor. "I have Impetus, Connor. I can make objects appear. Any object I can think of in detail, I can form out of nothing. My daughter can also do this... she's your age. She acted the same way you did when I explained all of this to her." Dr. Finn looked down at his display and held it towards his mouth. "Colonel, we have to go back."

"No..." Connor whispered.

"Hold on, Colonel," Dr. Finn spoke into his display. "You're sure, Connor? A promise is a promise."

"No, I... I... trust you," he responded as relief flowed over him like a crisp ocean wave.

"Good, then you better fasten yourself in tightly," he nodded to Connor looking towards the seat belt.

Connor scrambled to find which belt connected to which. He grasped at different ends like a cat with a string trying to make a match.

"Colonel... let's do hurry... we are running very late after all," Dr. Finn said with a smile on his face.

The whole car began to rumble, and the sound of machinery hummed all around them. Connor fastened the belt tightly just in time to notice that the car was leaving the ground. Connor put both hands on the window and glared as the earth left him underneath. He was in a hove rover and he couldn't believe it. His mouth opened and his eyes glowed with joy.

"The Colonel is a great pilot really," Dr. Finn leaned over to assure Connor. As the words left his lips, they flew into turbulence that made them drop several feet and jolt back and forth. "Well, most of the time anyhow."

"This is incredible!" Connor shouted.

"I'm very happy you think so, the last boy didn't fancy the ride and yakked on my shoes," he chuckled.

Connor laughed and looked back through the window.

"This ride will take a moment Connor, so you can get comfortable and take a nap if you'd like. I'm going to take one myself if that's quite alright," he mentioned.

"Ok sir," Connor replied.

Dr. Finn yawned and pressed another button near his console. His seat transformed into a reclined position. He punched another button as a tiny door opened and spat out a blanket. "I love the blanket button," he muttered as he turned over and became quite comfortable. Moments later, he was snoring and sleeping soundly.

Connor wasn't ready to sleep yet. He continued to look through the window and bask at the moment. He had never flown before. He wished that he could share every moment of this with his mom and dad. Unfortunately, they weren't there. He struggled for a while thinking about leaving his parents but felt that Dr. Finn was honest with him on why there was so much secrecy. He didn't want any harm to come to his parents. He wanted them to be safe. Connor sat back and enjoyed the flight.

Connor awoke to the sound of Dr. Finn making himself a glass of juice. Connor was leaning with his face on the door, and his face was hot as the sun hung directly above the car. He squinted his eyes, wiped his face, and turned towards the doctor.

Dr. Finn announced, "So you did sleep then? That's good. People need their rest dear boy."

"I guess I was more tired than I thought. Come to think of it... I didn't sleep at all last night," Connor replied.

"That's no surprise. I do apologize for all the stress but just know that you and your parents are safer this way," he continued.

Connor looked in the seat in front of him. It was facing him. The seat held his night light, the old manual, and the new model aircraft. He tilted his head and caught a sobering thought. Though this entire trip had been exhilarating thus far, Connor still didn't understand it all.

"Dr. Finn, I don't understand.... If this is all real, then what is my ability?" he asked.

"Well, Connor, I'm not quite sure. For some operators, their abilities aren't revealed until a bit later. It always happens in the 13th year though so don't fret. We'll most likely find out when we run tests even if you don't know," he explained.

"Operators? What's an operator?" Connor asked.

"Oh, you'll hear that more and more. That's what we call ourselves and people with Impetus. It sounds better than Impeturers, don't you think?" Dr. Finn chuckled.

"I suppose so. Well, where are we going?" Connor inquired.

"Now that is an excellent question young man," Dr. Finn sat his cup on the tray and spoke into his wrist display. "How long now, Colonel?" The tray began to rise and close itself like it had the last time.

"Five minutes," the Colonel's voice filtered through the display.

"Now if you'll look towards your right, Connor, you'll see your new home for the time being."

Connor looked through the glass window, and as the clouds parted, he saw a pyramid glistening in the sun. It was rotating and was the brightest white he'd ever seen. It had veins of light running along the sides. As they descended further, he noticed that the pyramid was actually hovering over a much larger structure. It was as if the top had been cut off and was rotating while the bottom part of the pyramid was standing still.

"What is it? Is it a spaceship?" Connor asked with excitement.

"Ha-ha, well technically I think it could be, but unless we start having operators born on the moon, then I suppose she'll stay around here," he responded.

"So it does move?"

"Yes, but it hasn't traveled anywhere in a very long time. It's called Eden. There are several hundred other people just like you who stay here for some time."

"I see," Connor said. "One last question."

"Fire away," Dr. Finn replied.

"Does Colonel Albert have any... Impetus... powers?"

"Hahaha! He does, Connor," Dr. Finn snickered.

A visor in the front of the car came down, and the Colonel looked back and smiled.

"Let's just say, he can hear very, very well," Dr. Finn suggested.

"Curious.... Then why all of the wrist display talking?" Connor asked.

"He loves to follow *protocol*."

Connor looked back towards the Colonel. The Colonel gave a quick salute and half sided smile.

"I see," Connor replied.

The car continued to decline in speed and height. It began to rumble much like it did before. Connor checked his seatbelt to make sure it was secure. He watched as the car landed into a small landing bay entering the side of the structure. As the car sped through the corridor, Connor placed a hand above his eyes to try to shade the bright lights flashing as they went by. Even with tinted windows, the lights were very, very bright.

The car came to a quick halt that gently lifted Connor forward from his seat. He heard a proper lady's voice over the intercom announce, "Hove rover 5 has arrived. You may exit the vehicle and enter the facility."

Dragon

Dr. Finn unbuckled and stepped out of the car. Connor also scrambled to unfasten himself so that he could keep up. He opened the door as quickly as he could and jumped out. He looked on as another car that seemed identical to his flew in on the other side of the landing bay. A familiar lady's voice rang out, "Hove rover 3 has arrived. You may exit the vehicle and enter the facility."

Connor stood still as he admired the area. He saw mechanical arms working above him in the smoothest of actions. The friction of gears didn't make a sound as the design seemed to be flawless. It was as if he had just entered a circus or magic show. He knew that factories and places like this could exist, but this was something else entirely. Connor spotted an older lady with gray and black frizzy hair standing in a room above him and towards the center of the structure. She wore tight dark robes and stood tall. She looked stiff. *That reminds me of Colonel Albert,* he thought.

A glass window separated he and the lady. He could see a desk, a tablet showing a recording, and a few white cushioned chairs alongside her. She stood as if she was on watch. Her view overlooked the landing bay which stretched longer than Connor's home street. It was a cloudy view showing the outside sky. She brought up a tiny cylinder device over her eye and looked towards Connor and then over to the other hove rover on the opposite side of him.

"Oh, Connor, don't forget your things," Dr. Finn said as he pointed inside the open car. Dr. Finn walked a few feet away walking closer to the other hove rover. As Connor grabbed his belongings, he noticed Colonel Albert walking in front of the car. Connor, with his hands full, turned his back to the open door and stepped backward to slam the door tight.

Colonel Albert stood to the side of the car as straight as an arrow watching Connor struggle to balance his belongings. Connor looked up and smiled as he dropped and quickly caught his night light before it hit the ground. The Colonel took his arm out in front of him and swung it to his side. His hand dropped down and slapped the front of the car twice. A large mechanical arm came down in an instant and hovered with a rectangular box a few feet above the car. The car lifted off the ground gracefully as the arm directed the vehicle to a track. The car was gently placed on the track. The track pulled the car into a black corridor and disappeared into the darkness. The arm quickly retracted back towards the tall ceiling while Connor was watching in awe.

Connor looked back around to notice Dr. Finn listening in on his wrist display. Connor couldn't make out what the voice was saying but heard Dr. Finn respond quite clearly.

"I'll be up shortly. Give me a few moments," he spoke into his wrist display. He walked back towards the Colonel and said, "Well that's the only other car that went out today. I'm going to check in, but I'll catch up with you later."

With a slightly lighter tone, he stepped over towards Connor. "Ok, Connor, you've been great so far, and now I'm going to leave you with the Colonel. He's going to help you get settled in and show you to your quarters. I'll catch up with you later." He then patted Connor on the back and started on his way. He strolled for a while past the other hove rover.

As he moved past, Connor noticed a tall man leave the driver seat of hove rover 3. The tall man wore a stylish suit with shiny shoes. He had a shadow of a beard and hair styled back.

He wore square brown glasses. He stretched the bottom of his suit jacket and stepped towards the back door of the car. He opened it and in the distance said, "Come along."

He stepped back and brushed his hand through his hair to make sure it was just so. Out of the car poured a young boy wearing a large jacket and heavy pants. He had on a purple knitted cap. He was dressed for much colder conditions than Connor. The tall man said, "Let me help you."

He bent over like a broken tree and grabbed the boy's cap and heavy coat. The boy wore a purple shirt hidden underneath the heavy coat that matched his cap. The tall man held the cap in one hand and the coat in the other. The boy dove back into the car for a moment and pulled out a doll. Connor could hardly see it in detail, but he noticed the doll with a tiny laser gun in its little hand.

Connor caught a glimpse of Dr. Finn leaving through a doorway past the scene. The tall stylish man closed the door and slapped the top of the car.

An identical process happened on the other side exactly as it did to Connor's car. The tall stylish man and the child were already on their way while the mechanical arm continued to move the car. The tall man and child skipped quickly and seemingly excited past Connor and the Colonel. They moved through a doorway on Connor's side of the landing bay.

"How long do you want to stand here?" the Colonel asked coldly.

"Oh, sorry, um... lead the way," Connor replied.

The Colonel walked ahead following the other two. Connor got a good hold on his belongings and hurried along behind him.

The Colonel and Connor entered a long hallway. There was no difference in the walls, ceiling, or floor. They were all tiled the same gray color. There were tiny lights tucked behind the wall tiles. They slowly pulsated and projected light as they traveled down the long, long hallway. Connor stepped to the right a bit to see past the Colonel, and he saw the tall man and child slow down and walk right as the hallway ended.

Connor hobbled along behind the smooth stepping Colonel. The hallway ended in front of them, but the corridor opened to his right down a matching hallway. He saw two black doors closing at the end that seemed to swallow the tall man and the other boy. As

Connor got closer, he saw that it was an elevator. The Colonel marched further. The doors opened, and they passed inside. The Colonel stood there, and Connor hung behind him closely.

"Repository," the Colonel said clearly.

The doors closed in front of them and the sound of air pushed underneath Connor's feet. They stood there motionless for only a few moments before the doors opened into another room entirely. "Did we even move?" Connor thought to himself. The elevator felt as if it stayed in one place.

They each made a stride out of the elevator. Connor detected a few individuals passing by in front of them wearing crimson robes. They were talking amongst themselves and seemed quite at home. The one in front was carrying a tablet. The room seemed rounded with a few other doorways. There were exotic plants and the sound of water flowing echoed. Plants hung from columns. Shrubbery was flourishing from half walls lined through the room. The surfaces of the walls and ceiling were white, and the room seemed clean, and the air was fresh. A young man and woman was sitting on a bench that aligned a half wall that housed yellow, red, and blue flowers. The petals hung with life, and the stems swayed lightly boasting the healthiest of green shades. The couple wore ocean blue robes. They each gave Connor a smile as he walked by trying to keep up with the Colonel.

As they walked on, Connor noticed the sound of water again but this time it was more prevalent. The Colonel's steps changed sounds briefly, and Connor noticed that they were now walking on a clear surface. Underneath him by a few feet was a rushing and gushing stream. It would pulse with force from time to time, and he could smell the water underneath him. He walked on but spun in a circle the best he could to see a beginning or ending to the river. He only saw an endless stream as his feet met an opaque surface once again. The smell and sound of water started to pass away, but the beauty of the plants continued onward.

They came along the end of the room, and the ceiling began to stretch even higher. There was a line of five square solid windows that stood just above the belly of Connor. A small console was to the right of each window. Connor stood back and to the right of the Colonel. The Colonel lifted his arm and pulled back his sleeve to find his wrist display. He held the wrist display in front of the console, and it flashed green. A number pad was then displayed and the Colonel stretched to touch it but glanced at Connor watching him. The Colonel slid in front of the console blocking Connor's view and continued to press the display.

The window shot open and revealed a belted surface.

"Place your items inside one at a time," the Colonel directed.

Connor, feeling hesitant, placed the new model aircraft on the surface through the opening. As he brought his hand back, the surface stole the item in the fastest of fashions.

"Where'd it go?!" Connor shouted.

"It's the Repository. It will hold your items and belongings until you need them again. You will be able to retrieve these items once you get your ornament," he explained as he pointed and tapped his wrist display.

"Ornament..." Connor replied. "Alright."

Connor placed the night light on the surface again and pulled his hand away. The surface seemed to devour the item before his eyes.

"Sir, it's traveling so fast, will it not break?" Connor questioned.

"All of the items will remain in their current condition," he said smugly as he looked at Connor holding the old manual under his arm.

Connor slowly pulled the manual from underneath his arm and with some reserve placed his father's gift onto the surface. It shot away and Connor, for the first time in a while, was empty handed.

Connor and the Colonel made their way back to the elevator. "Registration," said the Colonel.

Connor and the Colonel waited a moment in the elevator once again.

The door opened in an entirely new location. As Connor stepped out he noticed four children running in front of him. Two of them wore dark brown robes that seemed similar to the robes he'd seen so far. The other two children wore yellow robes. They all seemed playful and quite excited. Connor looked up to see a large round opening shining with a bright light downward. He looked up and tried to make out what was above but the light was very bright. The Colonel saw him looking upward and commented.

"That's the top you saw before we landed."

Connor looked harder and could see a slight surface churning in the sky miles above. "Oh, I see it now," he said.

"Careful around the railing," the Colonel said dryly as he started to march on.

In the center of the room was a round railing in which the light poured through. Connor stepped towards the railing and looked down. He was astonished at the distance underneath him. The light rested on a green surface. He could see tiny figures moving around vigorously on the surface. The green surface lay in the middle as four other small buildings sat around it.

"It's a field!" he said with excitement.

"Hurry up," the Colonel commanded.

The Colonel walked up to a desk that connected to another room. The desk divided the areas. Connor ran to catch up with the Colonel.

As Connor got closer to the desk, he caught a glimpse of a chunky man with a large bushy mustache.

He wore orange robes and his red hair whipped out like a dried out paint brush.

"Hey! Hey! Hey! A new recruit?" the man asked animatedly.

The Colonel winced and replied, "Yes, he needs an ornament."

"Oh, well welcome young operator!" he shouted with a jolly tone. "Let's see what we have here." He stepped away and started rummaging around out of Connor's sight. He hopped back up and sharply looked at Connor's wrist.

"Do step closer, boy. Let me see," the man said.

Connor stepped closer and raised his arm.

"Ah..." the man said as he wrapped measuring tape around his wrist." Could have sworn you were a seven!" he chuckled.

He stepped back out of view and continued to rummage. "So a 9 then! Hah!"

The colonel pointed to a tablet on the desk, and Connor put his hand up.

"Just rest your hand there," the Colonel instructed.

Connor placed his palm flat on the tablet.

"Ho! Ho!" the plump man shouted as he held an ornament high above his head. He placed it down on a small dish and began to log data on another tablet on his side of the desk.

"Alright, alright. Connor Laurel... 12 years of age.... Almost thirteen!" he cackled. "Ok, ok.... Ok, ok, ok.... Ok.... And.... Ok.... Ok, my boy you can lift your hand up. Now I do need you to enter a code. It's only 4 numbers, but you don't need to forget it! If you do, it could take weeks for you to get into your compartment!"

Connor thought for a moment. He was reminded of birthdays after the man mentioned his age. He thought about his parent's birthdays and the months in which they were born. He then saw the number display on the tablet. He quickly punched in the numbers 0802.

"Very good, very good," the happy man continued to click away. "Now, one last thing, what's your favorite animal?" he asked.

"My favorite animal? What?" Connor asked.

"We really need to move on," the Colonel moaned as if to be aggravated.

"Now, don't be a party pooper Colonel, you're just jealous you don't have an animal programmed into your ornament," he snapped back.

"Well?" the Colonel asked looking at Connor trying to get him to hurry along.

Connor was feeling rushed... furthermore, never owned a pet. He wasn't sure which animal he liked. He never really thought about animals often.

"Come on now son, we don't want the Colonel to get into a tizzy," the funny man egged him on.

Connor said the first thing that came to his mind. "Draken..." he mumbled while in deep thought.

"Speak up boy! What now? Hehehe!"

Connor began to look up. "Draken... drake.... Dragon! Yes... Dragon... Sir."

"Dragon?! Ho! Ho! Now that's a new one. I've never given someone a *mythical* creature like that."

"Do hurry, Walterrrr..." the Colonel pleaded.

"Alright, alright… I'm done," he clicked frantically. Walter grabbed the device up and placed it around Connor's arm, and it snapped on automatically.

"Good day, Walter," the Colonel said as he turned and walked on.

"And to you, my resolute friend," he said giggling and saluting the Colonel to his back.

Connor waved and shouted, "Thanks!" He started to jog to catch up with the Colonel.

"Just whisper dragon into the ornament, and the program will start up! It will only obey your voice!" Walter yelled. Connor looked back and waved again as he kept pace.

Connor found himself in the elevator yet again, but this time he had an ornament.

Chest

"Rotunda," said the Colonel.

As the doors opened, Connor looked upon the most impressive view yet. The walls were reaching five stories high. A dome ceiling hung above him. In the concave ceiling, there were projections of a woman giving announcements. Onlookers could view the image at the same angle from any part of the room. The room was bustling with movement. People were walking in all directions. As Connor looked back, he saw a row of matching elevators with people arriving and others leaving. There were escalators and well-lit signs stating where the corridors led. One read *Infirmary* boasted a bright red and white cross. Another straight ahead read *Assembly*. There was also a large corridor that read *Analysis*.

"You'll be spending a lot of time there," the Colonel pointed towards the Analysis hall.

"Why, sir?"

"All new operators have to be tested early on," he explained.

Suddenly Connor felt a slight vibration running up his arm. He looked down, and the ornament was vibrating gently. He brought it closer to see it. "Please proceed to the Assembly Hall," it announced. Connor held it out in front of him, and a green arrow was displayed pointing towards the Assembly corridor. As he moved his arm, the arrow tilted towards the hall at every angle. It was like a compass but only pointing to the area, he was directed to go.

"Neat," he said.

He looked up and watched again as the Colonel was no longer standing there. He looked back towards the elevator to see the Colonel standing inside. "Be well, Connor. Reserves." The doors closed and the Colonel was gone. Connor stepped towards the door about to say something, but it was too late. He turned back around, took a deep breath, and made his way towards the Assembly Hall.

Connor passed through the large corridor. It opened into a foyer with two doorways on each side and a staircase on the left. Connor could hear a muffled voice coming through the doors. He opened the left door and walked through. Once inside he caught a glimpse of a large stage and several rows of empty seats.

Above him were two extra floors of seats descending towards the stage.

To his surprise, the voice he heard was the amplified voice of Dr. Finn.

"Having said that, if no one has welcomed you let me say, Welcome to Eden! Oh.... Hello, Connor, please find a seat wherever you're comfortable," the doctor directed.

There were hundreds of empty seats but only twelve or thirteen other children were spread out in different sections and towards the front. They all looked back at Connor as Dr. Finn pointed him out. Connor noticed that one of them was the child who arrived next to him in the landing bay. They all continued to watch him as he made his way down the aisle. There were four long aisles and four large sections. The seats were cushioned with a green fabric that matched a steady green curtain that held still far above the doctor on stage. The walls were dimly lit reminiscent of the gray hall he had traveled through earlier. The stage glowed brighter than the rest of the room but Connor didn't see any lights illuminating it. He walked down while all eyes locked on him. He quickly sat down on the left most row, three seats inward.

"Very good then, as I was saying… welcome. By now you all know why you're here and why it's important for you to be here rather than at your home. This facility will test your mind and abilities so that you can be strong and healthy but also be in complete control of who you are. One of man's worst fears is to be himself but all the while not *know* himself. At Eden, you will do both, I assure you. As you may have guessed, our facility is a secret. Though it is large in size, it is hidden from the general public of the world. Leaders from the Coalitions know of our existence and support our efforts. With that knowledge, it is imperative that we keep this place a secret. It would be terribly dangerous if your parents and loved ones knew about this place. Word could easily get out about our existence. Before Eden, our kind were scared and constantly fighting for their lives. In time, we will train you to control yourself so that you can go back to your respective lands and live happy and healthy lives. Some of you, like myself, may decide or be selected to stay here to help future generations. As the numbers of new operators decrease every year, it is important that we continue to support and grow with one another. Now, none of you will be able to communicate with the outside world for at least a month. We need to make sure that you fully understand the rules and regulations. If for whatever reason any of us decided to divulge our system to common folk, then there would be a severe penalty put in place. However, it has been years since the last time we had an offense and discipline was enforced. So I'm sure we won't need to worry about that from any of you."

Connor looked around the room as the doctor continued. All of the children were wearing their native clothing. There were no robes to be seen. He noticed one child seemingly excited. A child in a different seat looked rather sad. It was no surprise to him because he felt quite torn about the entire situation.

"Some of you have already discovered your ability and may have even used it in front of your friends or family. There's no need to be alarmed. We have taken every necessary action to ensure an explanation for each and every case. Now, the ones of you who have shown an ability, you will receive a yellow robe. Ok... I would like to take a moment to welcome my lovely assistant."

He opened up his hand and stretched his arm to the right side of the stage. A young girl with straight golden hair walked out from the side. Her robe was yellow and new. She had a large smile, a tiny nose, and green eyes. She walked with confidence but stumbled a bit during her strut across the stage. A few children snickered as she recovered.

"Now, show us what you can do young lady!" Dr. Finn said playfully.

The girl lifted her right arm in the air, and suddenly a small mass started to grow and shape in her hand. Within an instant, she was holding an orange ball. It was no bigger than her fist yet it demanded applause. The children stood up and clapped their hands as she took a proud bow. She threw the ball out of the stage, and one of the kids in the audience caught it. The child was amazed as he examined this astounding power. Connor was reminded of Samantha's orange balloon. *She would love this place,* he thought to himself as he cracked a smile.

The girl on stage took a bow, and Dr. Finn bowed with her.

"Go and sit by Connor, dear. He looks far too lonely over there," Dr. Finn suggested.

The girl walked to the side of the stage from whence she came.

"Some of you may not have an ability yet, or you may have one, and you don't know what it is. Regardless, you will be assigned a dark brown robe. Now the colors do not mean that anyone is better than anyone. It's only a way for us to be able to keep up with everyone!" he chuckled.

"You no doubt have seen different color robes on different people. These are different colors assigned for development of abilities and achievements. Older people will almost always have a different color robe from your own. All of you are either thirteen or about to be thirteen. Well… we… we don't have my 14-year-olds here, do we?"

No one raised his or her hands or spoke up.

"I didn't think I smelled any 14-year-olds," the professor joked.

A few children snickered at the poor joke. At that moment, Connor noticed the girl from the stage walking down the aisle behind him. She sat down in the seat next to him near the aisle.

"You're his daughter," Connor said.

"Why, yes, how did you know?" she asked.

"He told me that you could do that."

"Do what???"

"Make... stuff," Connor replied.

"Oh, yes, I'm Natalie... Natalie Finn," she introduced herself and held out her hand.

Connor grasped her hand, "It's a pleasure."

"When we're done with this meeting, your ornaments will direct you to the Reserves. There you will be shown to your bunk. After that, you'll see where you'll be eating. It's approaching dinner time in fact. You will receive information about your schedule for the next few days as well. Before we dismiss, are there any questions?" he asked.

A child raised his hand. "Um, yes son?"

A child asked, "When will we be able to go home again?"

"Well, that depends, most of our newer operators will visit their home in April but possibly not until August. Each person is different. You will all be able to go home for the holidays, however," he answered clearly. "Anyone else?"

The room paused and right as he was about to conclude the meeting, Connor slipped his hand up high.

"Yes, Connor, what is it?"

"Sir, what is the floating structure above us?" he inquired.

A child two rows up resounded, "Yeh," as if to second the question.

"Now, that is an excellent question. That is our most advanced system. It houses a mainframe that actually allowed us to find each and every one of you. It even found me!" he said in a positive tone. "It is most commonly known as the Edifice."

Connor and the other children seemed satisfied with the answer.

"Alright, well then, I guess that concludes our meeting. I hope to bump into each of you again soon," Dr. Finn concluded.

He took a bow and headed off the stage. Moments later, each student felt a vibration on their arms. They each checked their ornaments. "Please head to the elevators," the message read aloud on Connor's ornament.

"I'll walk with you. This place is rather large," Natalie explained.

"Thanks."

They each rose from their seats and trailed the other children as they exited the Assembly hall.

"So, your dad lives here?" Connor asked as they walked through the corridor back into the Rotunda.

"Basically, he's been here most of his life. He was chosen to help with Eden, and he accepted," she explained.

"Oh, ok. Do you ever leave here? Ya know, go somewhere else when everyone else is gone?"

"I've only been here for three weeks actually. It's kind of new to me. I live with my aunt when I'm not here," she stated.

"Aren't you confused? I mean, I just feel clueless. None of this feels real or normal," Connor discussed.

They began to pass along under the dome in the Rotunda.

"Well, my father would visit me often. He always explained that he was at work at a medical facility. When I started getting my powers, I just sort of *knew*. My aunt doesn't know though. She still thinks we are in a medical facility," she explained.

"Your dad lied to you though," Connor countered.

"I suppose he did. That did hurt my feelings, but… once I saw what he could do, it made sense to me. He was always calling me as I grew up. I never really felt alone. I'm just glad I have him now. Some kids don't have parents at all! That's what my aunt says anyways," Natalie continued.

"So where is your mom? Is she a doctor too?" he asked thinking that he would meet her soon.

"My mom died actually," she replied.

Connor apologized, "OH, I'm very sorry. I didn't know."

"It's ok. I never really knew her, you see. She died when she gave birth to me. It's quite sad for my dad. It can also make me sad if I think about it too much," she said with emotion.

"I didn't mean to make you sad."

"It's ok, I'm fine…" she said as she looked at him. Connor stared back to make sure she was fine. "I mean it. Don't worry," she responded brightly and smiled.

They stepped into the elevator. "Reserves," she spoke.

The doors closed and they were on their way.

The black doors opened, and they stepped out into a hallway. A hallway led to the left and one to the right. There was also a hallway down the center. The walls were white, and veins of light ran through the walls. It was clean, and the air was cool to the skin.

"Ok, so to the left are the bunks and living quarters. That's where your robes will be. Everyone is assigned a chest as well."

"A chest?" he asked

"Yes, like a box for your stuff," she replied.

"The hall to the right is the café. That's where we eat our meals. And down the middle will lead you to the common rooms for studying, playing, talking, etc. If you go down the center you can eventually get to the bunks and the café. The lavatories are also there for showers and... well you know."

"Nice," Connor confirmed.

"It's almost dinner time, so I'm going to the café. You can find me there if you'd like," she said as she started walking down the right hallway.

"Ok, sounds great!" he stated.

He looked both ways and then made his way down the left hallway. He took a glimpse at his ornament, and a green arrow pointed onward.

He turned a corner and noticed an open doorway to a room with beds. The room was square and had several beds. Each bed had a white headboard that seemed adjustable. On the ceiling was a large display. Above him looked like a blue sky with puffy white clouds. It was warm but not overly distracting. The walls were light gray and simple. Each bed had a box with a display on the front slit where the box opened. Some chests were yellow, and some were dark brown. There was one bed at the end of the room that had folded dark brown robes lying on it. Next to this bed was a white chest. Connor continued along the room and came across the bed. These were Connor's assigned robes. The display on the box by the bed read, "Laurel, Connor" and a number pad was underneath the name. Connor remembered his number and quickly entered

0802. The box started to glimmer. The box slowly transformed into a brownish color as the white hue vanished.

Pop! Click! Pop!

The box opened and to Connor's surprise, he saw his manual, aircraft model, and night light lying at the bottom. They were resting on a few extra folded brown robes. He picked up the model and thought that he might wake up from a dream at any moment. "How is any of this possible?" he pondered. He placed the model back in the box and closed the top. He heard it lock and the color remained brown.

Before picking up the robe, he decided to move the box to the end of the bed. He tried to pull on it, but it wouldn't budge. He heard a group coming down the hallway, but he kept working. He got on the opposite side and tried to push it with all of his might.

"Look at this kid!" someone announced.

Laughter rang out among the group. Connor stopped pushing and stood up straight. He saw three boys and two girls wearing yellow robes.

"Are you dense?! Those don't move, dummy!" the adolescent scoffed. The others continued to giggle and snicker.

The front boy had a sharp chin and mischievous smile. He had straight pitch black hair that tucked behind each ear.

"Good one, Dominic," a boy in the back of the group muttered.

Connor felt embarrassed and wanted to lash out. He was about to spout back when he heard someone step up behind him. He turned around to find a teen wearing yellow robes. He was a decent bit taller than Connor. He had short Curly hair with a honey tint. He showed a few crooked teeth but had a stern look on his face.

"Didn't I see you harassing your box a few months ago, Youuuu-----GENE!" the yellow robed teen threatened.

"You wish, you dud... let's go I'm starving," Dominic commanded his crew. They walked on, and Connor felt slightly vindicated.

"I saw his middle name last year on his ornament. It's nice to remind everyone what a dimwit he is from time to time. I'm Liam Hudson," the boy said as he reached out with his hand.

Connor took his hand firmly and shook it. "I'm Connor, by the way, where did you come from?"

"Oh, there's a doorway that leads to a small lavatory and closet. I was changing into a fresh robe. Don't worry about him though; he's a rat if I'm honest," Liam joked.

Connor grinned with approval and from his stomach came a prudent grumble.

"Hungry, friend?" Liam assumed.

"Yeh, I guess I am. Come to think of it; I haven't eaten since early this morning."

"Well, you're in luck. I think we're having willow potato soup for dinner. It's very tasty."

"I actually really like potatoes!" Connor answered.

Liam waited around for a moment as Connor went into the closet and changed into his robes. They felt a bit long, but the fit was perfect on his chest and waist. He straightened the garb out, made a quick stretch, and walked back into the bunk room.

"Simply stunning," Liam teased.

"Ah, bite me," Connor fired back.

They each laughed and roamed into the hallway and chatted as they walked toward the café.

They came to the opening of the café' and the aroma of fresh food tickled Connor's nose. *I hope I can go for seconds,* he thought.

Teens and adults were going down a line getting their food as clean mechanical arms placed bowls and cups onto an inviting conveyor belt. There wasn't only the willow potato soup but an assortment of desserts, beverages, and an eclectic selection of meats and vegetables. Feel good music showered the room at a modest volume. They made their way to the food and Connor asked, "So you're 14 then?"

"No, I'm only 13," he replied.

"Oh, well, you just mentioned that you and Dominic were here last year."

"Oh right, I see, no... I came right before the summer because my birthday is in late winter. People come in year round if they start using their abilities, but they try to keep everything going on a schedule. It can get confusing, but it all seems to work out," Liam babbled.

As they began to pick up their trays, they heard a voice launch across the room. "Liam!" They searched with their eyes to find the source. Liam waved at a teen in an ocean blue robe, and he waved back. Connor assumed it was a friend of his that he made last year.

"That's my cousin. Most people don't have any family members here," he added. "It was a real shame when he first left. It was three years ago. My mom cried, and I was eaten up by it as well. We thought he was sick," Liam continued. "Turns out, we're the lucky ones."

"I suppose you're right. This place is magnificent," Connor responded.

"I agree."

"Hey, there's Natalie," Connor pointed out.

"Oh, you're um... girlfriend eh???" Liam grinned.

"Ha-ha, I only just arrived, pal. Her dad brought me here. She showed me to the bunks… I hardly know her," Connor explained.

"Now that you mention it, I think I have seen her once or twice. Shall we?"

"Sure." Connor led the way.

They passed by several rows of tables. The table tops all glowed with different colored lights underneath that would cycle from time to time. They arrived at Natalie's pink table, and each plopped down.

"Hi, Natalie. This is Liam," Connor introduced him.

"Hi," Liam greeted her with an awkward handshake over his tray and hers alike.

"Oh," she looked uncomfortable as part of his robe sat on the edge of her bowl. "Nice to meet you, Liam," she said quickly and shook his hand hoping he would pull it back. They began to eat, and Connor was eating at an exceptional rate. Natalie beckoned, "Don't get sick, Connor."

"Sorry. I'm just really hungry," he said.

He slowed down a bit but kept a quicker pace than the others. Connor finished the bowl quickly and asked them if he could get a second bowl. They nodded yes, and he went back to the line. After he grabbed another bowl, he saw two adults talking in the corner. One of the ladies was staring at him and wasn't breaking eye contact. He crept on uncomfortably. As he marched back towards his table, he got a better glimpse of the lady. It was the same lady who watched him in the landing bay from the room up above.

As he arrived back at the table, Natalie and Liam were talking, and the table was lime green. Natalie held her hand over her tray near her spoon and produced an exact replica under her palm. "That's terrific!" Liam obliged. She handed him the spoon.

"Well, what can you do? You have yellow robes after all," she questioned him.

"Oh yeah," Liam replied as if he forgot that he could do anything. "My mom took me to the hospital probably four times before I came here. Everyone thought it was a fever," Liam reached over and touched Connor's bowl for a moment. He looked intently at the bowl, and the liquid started to bubble and boil.

"Hot! That's heat!" Connor uttered.

"That's right... I heat up I suppose," Liam replied.

"Wow that is impressive," Natalie chimed.

Connor quickly started to feel left out after he only just began to fit in. Rumbling dishes quaked down the row as Connor caught sight of a large silly man carrying a mountain of cake and pie on his tray. As he bounced closer, Connor realized that it was the man who gave him his ornament. "Hey, mister!" Connor spoke up as he was about to bustle by.

"Why hello, Connor!" he clucked.

"Hi. Mr. Templeton," Natalie muttered.

"Oh my, didn't see you there Natalie!" he replied. He edged his way onto the table almost sitting on Natalie. Her tray and her body were pushed down the bench like a ragdoll as he made his way down.

"Templeton??? Colonel Albert called you Walter at the registration room," Connor mentioned.

"Walter Templeton! That's my name, hik-hik," he laughed with a cheek full of pie.

"Yes, yes... I've known Daniel for many years now."

"Who's Daniel?" Liam chimed in.

"Colonel Daniel Albert," he replied.

"He didn't mention his first name I guess. He's always down to business. You've experienced his *no-nonsense* attitude, eh, Connor?" Mr. Templeton implied.

They watched as the jolly ginger man plowed his way through a horde of sweets. Connor looked back over his shoulder and saw the woman still looking his way. The thought came to him to ask Mr. Templeton about her.

"How's the dolphin, Ms. Finn?" Walter asked as he took a big swallow.

"She's fine, she did wake me up with her squeaking last night. I must have called her in my sleep," Natalie explained.

"Well let's have a look."

She lifted her ornament, and a projection of a small pool climbed up from the device. It was filled with water, and a tiny dolphin sprung out of the digital pond and turned a flip before diving back down. Mr. Templeton reached his finger over as to pet the dolphin on its tiny nose lightly. The dolphin responded with a little squeak. Mr. Templeton then took in a deep breath as they looked at him perplexed. He let out the breath with his lips rounded tightly towards the digital cup. The water began to wake, and waves crashed as the dolphin struggled to fight the sudden current. Natalie quickly pulled the ornament away and put it by her side as the projection disappeared.

"Batten down the hatches!" Templeton snickered playfully.

Liam chuckled.

Connor asked, "Mr. Templeton, who's that lady over there?"

The jolly man leaned over and squinted his eyes to see. Natalie and Liam spied the fuzzy haired lady as well.

"That's Malinda Marks. General Malinda Marks. She runs the show around here. If anyone ever has a problem they go to her," Mr. Templeton explained.

"Well, she seems to be taking a great interest in Connor here," Liam replied.

"Seems like it," Natalie confirmed.

Templeton began to engulf his last pastry on the tray as Liam asked, "So, what's your Impetus ability?"

"Isn't it obvious? I can eat all I want and never get fat!" he kept a straight face.

The children seemed perplexed as they were staring at an overly hefty individual. His lips started to squeak and stutter as he began to laugh deeply and uncontrollably.

"I'm only kidding!" he shouted as he patted Natalie on the back. The taps felt more like a slap to her smaller frame as her hair flung in front of her face. Liam saw her discomfort and snickered.

"I am the Eden tinkerer for a reason. I can see the script and coding of your devices, of several devices. I do have to focus though. Understanding your ornaments is one thing but controlling it is something else. You have to coax them with a smooth language to get them to work how you want. Like your dolphin, Ms. Finn," he explained. Mr. Templeton finished his last bite and wished them farewell.

They each took their trays back to the conveyor belt and headed back down the corridor. Natalie told them bye and headed down the hall a bit further to the female quarters. The boys turned back to their room and started to settle in. Connor let out a long yawn.

"You're tired?" Liam asked.

"I'm especially tired it seems," Connor replied lying on his bed in pajamas. Liam was in the bed across from him. Only two other boys had gotten ready for bed.

"I just don't get it..." Connor murmured.

"Get what?"

"Well earlier today, I was with Colonel Albert. I left my things in his repository. But when I opened the box, my things were inside. Why didn't he just bring them down here? Why did he lock them up, get them out, and bring them back later?" Connor asked.

"That sounds exhausting..." Liam groaned. "Check this out, my poorly adjusted friend." Liam hopped up from his bed and bent over his box. Connor sat up to examine him.

Liam unlocked his box and opened it. Liam searched around the room a bit. He went into the closet and came back out with a shoe. He signaled Connor to walk over to his box. Connor slipped out of bed and crawled over. Liam dropped the shoe in the box and closed it tight. Once it locked, he went on, "Now that it's closed, I can do this." He placed his finger on the top of his yellow lit box, and a digital interface appeared.

Connor watched closely.

Messages began to appear.

Send item?

Liam could choose to press *yes* or *cancel*

He clicked *yes*.

The last added item?

He clicked *yes* again.

"If I had clicked cancel, then it would have asked me to send all items. I doubt anyone would want to do that," he explained.

Enter a name showed up on the display.

A tiny digital keyboard appeared, and he typed in *Connor Laurel.*

Accepted popped up with a green check mark.

More messages appeared.

Send or *Cancel.*

Liam pressed *Send.*

"Ok, we're done," Liam said as he pointed to Connor's chest. Within 5 seconds a line of white light ran across the top of Connor's chest. He looked back at Liam inquisitively.

"Go on. Go open it," Liam waved his arms towards the box.

Connor punched in his code, unlatched the box, and found the shoe inside with his other belongings.

"Incredible!" he shouted.

"Shhhhh," a boy from a few beds down hissed.

Liam explained, "If you miss the first line of light in your box, it'll light back up every 10 minutes to remind you to open it and receive whatever's inside."

Connor closed the box and handed the shoe over to Liam. Liam put the shoe in its rightful place, and they each crawled back into bed.

"That's how he did it!" Liam whispered loudly.

Connor gave him a thumbs up and said, "Goodnight."

He tucked his sheets over him, looked up at the ceiling as it displayed a cloudy dark sky, and he slowly drifted to sleep.

Inspiration

Buzzzzz.... Buzzzz.... Buzz....

Connor was woken by a vibration on his arm. He looked at his ornament, and it showed 7:30 AM and continued to vibrate.

"Awake," Liam said with a raspy voice speaking into his ornament. Liam sat up from his bed and stretched his arms. Connor repeated the command into his own ornament, "Awake," and the vibration subsided.

The ceiling projected a rising sun that calmly invigorated the room. All of the boys down the row of beds began to sit up stretching and yawning. It was if they were digging their way out of quicksand. They stumbled around and stretched their legs while the ceiling began to play a recording. A projection of General Marks came down.

"Good morning, I trust you all slept well. Please refrain from going to the Repository if at all possible. We will be performing extra maintenance today, and we ask that you do not go there as it may hinder the process. Also, we will be beginning basic studies and training next week, so if you haven't, please go to the

References floor and download your required materials. Finally, we will be having spiced chicken with sweet greens for dinner. Be well," the voice of the General concluded. The recording ended, and the ceiling returned to the sunrise.

The boys all got up, got clean, and dressed in their robes for the day.

"Please proceed to room 7 in Analysis Hall," Liam's ornament echoed.

"I guess I'll be on my way then," he nodded to Connor. He followed the arrow on his ornament out into the hallway.

"Please proceed to the References floor," Connor's ornament instructed.

He lifted the ornament and followed the arrow to the elevator.

He got into an elevator and was then joined by Dominic before the doors could close. He attempted to beat down the memory of being teased by this rude individual yesterday. "Good morning," Connor greeted.

Dominic didn't acknowledge the greeting and commanded, "Rotunda," the doors closed. They opened again, and as Dominic took a stride outward, he murmured, "Suck an egg," back at Connor.

Connor felt annoyed and clinched his fist. "References," he scowled. The doors closed and he was on his way. As the doors opened, Connor confidently stepped out into a rectangular room with lines of digital servers and computing parts. They stood tall reaching two stories high. Each section had a mechanical lift that operators could stand on to reach the higher areas. Several other operators were walking around and examining the lines of servers. The room was crisp white but felt warm from all of the working hardware. His ornament pointed him down a row. When he got close to the destination, he heard, "Downloading. Now."

He watched as his ornament showed the progress of digital material being downloaded to his display. There was a download bar and above it read *Physics*. After the download had completed, he was directed to walk further down the row. Another download began. *Trigonometry* was displayed. He was starting to get nervous that hard work was in his near future. He kept going. The process repeated again and again. *Biology... Sociology.... Combative Training....* He froze.

"Is this a mistake?" he mumbled.

"No, no it isn't," a voice declared.

Connor jumped a bit as he was quite startled by the mysterious man's voice from behind him. He turned around to see who was speaking. The man brushed his hand through his clean, stylish hair. Connor remembered the man from the landing bay. He was in the other hove rover and took the other boy into Eden.

"Looks like you will be learning to defend yourself," he smiled confidently. "Sorry to frighten you. I noticed you over here, and I thought I'd introduce myself. You were at the landing bay yesterday, right?" the man inquired.

"Um, yes. Yes, that was me. I'm Connor," he recovered.

"Greetings, Connor. Benjamin Ozil, I'm a teacher here," he announced with dignity.

He placed his hand on Connor's shoulder. "I'll see you in class." Then he walked off as smoothly as possible while whistling a tune.

Connor became excited. He scurried down to the next area to find the next download. *Group Based Tactics....* He was exploding with energy and couldn't stop smiling. He ran further down as fast as he could. His ornament scanned... *Aviation.* Connor could only imagine what was going to happen and why he would need these digital books. He felt ready for any challenge and raced back towards the elevator. His ornament sounded off, "Please proceed to Analysis hall." He couldn't wait. He hopped on the elevator and shouted, "Rotunda" as if he just won a match or defeated a foe. *This all kind of seems violent... Why am I so wired?* he thought.

The doors flew open, and with a nice trot, he continued to the Analysis corridor. He passed by several young operators in yellow and brown robes entering rooms within the Analysis area. Connor looked at his ornament, and it kept pointing straight ahead. He walked for a few minutes until he reached the end of the corridor. In front of him was a much smaller opening. It read *Dr. Finn's Office* above the archway. He proceeded.

Connor entered Dr. Finn's office. He observed Dr. Finn turned around reading his tablet while facing a window. The window overlooked the outside edge of the structure and was very bright. The sun was reflecting off the surface. Connor could see far into the distance as a dark rain cloud sailed across the sky. There was a sleek green desk and a comfy chair to match. A projected image of Natalie was at the corner of this desk and was slightly tilted up for everyone to see. To Connor's right stood a shelf with dozens and dozens of tablets. On the other side of the room, his coat hung on a metal rack, and small conveyor belt stuck out of the wall. Connor stood behind two black chairs on the guest side of the desk.

"Hi, doctor," Connor greeted him pleasantly.

"Hello, Connor! I didn't see you come in, please take a seat," Dr. Finn asked kindly.

Connor replied with exhilaration, "I'd be delighted!"

The doctor looked at him slightly confused as this was not a normal response. Before Connor could sit down, two students with Green robes barged in. "Dr. Finn, Henry broke two chairs in our room."

"That Henry..." he replied. "Ok, take those and tell him to be careful!" he shouted as they took the chairs and ran out.

Connor stood there.

The doctor looked at him, "Oh right," he waved his hand, and an identical black chair appeared in front of Connor. Dr. Finn made a kind gesture inviting him to sit finally. "Connor, your first bit of time here at Eden may bore you. It's part of the process, however.

Today, you're going to be lying back on a chair for hours," he said regrettably.

"That's amazing, sir! I really can't wait to get started!" Connor oozed with anticipation.

The doctor sat in his chair and placed his hand on his chin. He glared at Connor with a puzzled look in his eye. Connor just gazed back and smiled.

Dr. Finn slowly changed his face and a feeling of relief and realization wrapped around him.

"Haha," he chuckled and stood up. He walked around to the front of the desk and leaned onto his desk in front of Connor. He crossed his arms and looked down at him. "Connor, did you by chance run into Professor Ozil this morning?"

"Yes! I met him down in Resources!"

Dr. Finn questioned, "Did he shake your hand?"

Connor, still excited, but confused by the question replied, "No, but he did pat me on the shoulder."

"I knew it..." Dr. Finn nodded. "Connor, Professor Ozil's ability is to inspire those around him. It's especially strong when he touches you. You'll find it a bit sobering now that you realize that. It actually makes him a sharp professor. Children are more interested in his lectures. I wouldn't worry though; he doesn't abuse it. This was probably a comical initiation of sorts."

Connor continued to smile and suddenly understood why he was so thrilled at the thought of sitting still in a chair for hours.

"This first scan is important. We want you to stay in the room during the entire process. Once the scan starts, it won't stop for a while. You may want to visit a lavatory before you head in," the doctor suggested.

"Will it hurt?" Connor asked with a goofy smile.

"Only if a mind numbing experience hurts you, my boy," Dr. Finn joked. He stepped towards the shelf with the tablets and thumbed through them. "I'll send your issued tablet to your chest. You really won't need it until next week. However, if you're the studious type, you can start reading later today to prepare for classes next week. It was nice seeing you again, Connor. But you should probably run along."

"Ok, sir." Connor stood up, took a bow, and walked outside. He looked down at his ornament, and it was directing him to walk back along the corridor. He went on until he found the right room. Room 22. He walked in and saw only a single reclined chair in the middle of the room. The door closed behind him automatically. His ornament spouted, "Please sit down and remain seated. Get comfortable and relax."

Connor climbed onto the chair. It was dark brown like his robe and rather comfortable. The lights in the walls all went out, and the room went dark. A light began to shine above him. It resembled moonlight and was calm to endure. Hours passed, and Connor kept a soft smile on his face.

Connor's arm vibrated. "Proceed to the Reserves," his ornament suggested. Connor had been in that room all morning. He got a single hour break in which he grabbed a sandwich from the café. He ate alone and came back to the room to continue.

He sat back down for another five hours. Later, his ornament beckoned him to go and eat once again. He passed by a few brown robed operators on his way through the Rotunda. They all seemed to be headed for the Reserves. Connor arrived in the café and grabbed a spiced chicken tray. He moved through the café and spotted Liam waving at him from a coral colored table. Connor sat down and greeted him.

"How was your day?" Liam asked.

"Boring... I sat in a chair all day. Supposedly I was being scanned. It felt like nothing happened," Connor explained. "However, Professor Ozil did use his ability on me. That was a new experience."

"That's bonkers! I heard he could do that but wasn't sure if it were true. I figured girls just swooned over him for his looks or something," he joked.

"No, it was very real; I was ready to take on anything, even trigonometry!" Connor laughed.

"Yikes," Liam confirmed.

Connor caught sight of Natalie grabbing a tray and flagged her over. She obliged.

"But what about you? What did you do all day?" Connor asked.

"I was just in a room with random objects. I was directed to heat the items. It was pretty dull really. I did melt a wax candle without lighting it. So that's something," Liam replied.

Natalie sat down and let out a large sigh. "If I have to make another cup I may vomit."

Liam covered his plate with his arms shielding it from her and asked, "What?!"

"I had to make so many cups today. I don't mind making a cup, but it was… make a wood cup, make a plastic cup, make a tall cup, make a short cup, make a red cup, make a blue cup," She rambled.

"Yikes," Liam said again.

The table shifted colors to a glistening black.

"Well, at least you have an ability and can use it. I'm not even a real operator yet," Connor replied.

Natalie looked down at her tray and felt a little guilty. "I'm sorry, Connor. I shouldn't complain. I'm sure your ability will present itself any day now."

Liam added, "Yeh, it's only a matter of time. I mean, you're not even 13 yet, technically."

"I guess that's true," Connor answered.

They continued to eat their food and talk. A few minutes later, Liam piped up. "Ya know, this spiced chicken really is spicy. I can handle heat, but this has its own source of power, if you know what I mean." He blew air out of his mouth in front of him in an attempt to cool his mouth. The heat from the exhale slapped Connor as it passed by.

It reminded him of his favorite show *Draken*. Draken could breathe fire and Liam made a similar posture as Draken would often do in the show during those moments.

"Oh... oh.... Yeh..." Connor uttered.

"What?" Natalie asked.

"I almost forgot," he held up his ornament closely to his mouth and whispered, "Dragon."

Instantly a loud roar came crashing through his ornament, and it caused several people around him to stop and look his way. He was seemingly embarrassed as his ornament projected an image of a mighty orange dragon climbing out of a rock bed and breathing fire three feet above his ornament. The beast was acting loudly and hovering as it flapped its wings.

"How do I make it stop?!" Connor panicked.

"Just put your arm down," Natalie instructed.

Connor quickly put his arm down and blushed. Eyes from all over the room drifted away from him as they went back to their eating and conversations.

"Holy moly... I'm glad that doesn't happen instead of the regular alarm in the morning. I think you'd croak before you ever found your Impetus, Connor," Liam joked as the three laughed for a while.

They finished eating and put their trays away. They continued talking in one of the common rooms connected to the bunks. It was a basic clean lobby with sofas and couches. Young operators would go there to read their tablets, play digital games, or simply get together. They spoke with others and tried to guess how much Mr. Walter Templeton weighed. Time passed on, and their ornaments directed them to bed. They went to sleep soundly, and the next morning they received announcements.

For four days, Connor and the others went through a similar process. Connor was growing frustrated about sitting for long hours but was relieved that his dragon could come out during the scan. He taught the dragon a few commands and learned how to play with it. He also trained it to make a more quiet entrance.

He appropriately named the dragon, Draken. He imagined how great it would be if the dragon would turn into his favorite fictional character. Draken could be his sidekick in this new place. Draken always knew what to do in every situation. Connor loved his confidence on the show. In an accepting sigh, he spoke, "I'm ok with you just being a dragon though." He petted the small dragon as it invited him to keep doing so. Connor stretched his neck and looked back up at the glowing light above him in the dark room and rested his ornament by his side.

<u>Trouble</u>

Connor was relieved two days later. It was an off day, and that meant no extra-long sitting. He and Liam made their way to the common rooms. There they found Natalie playing chess on a tablet with a girl from her bunk. They gave her a quick wave but moved on through the hallways. Connor and Liam were walking and talking without paying attention. Suddenly another person bumped into Connor causing him to stumble a bit. "Grrr…" Connor rumbled. It was Dominic. Dominic and another yellow robed boy sneered at them as they entered the elevator. They rolled their eyes and continued. "Repository," Liam spoke.

They arrived at the Repository, and it smelled as fresh and inviting as before. The aroma from the plants bathed them. They were greeted with a slight breeze gifted by the rushing water underneath. All of the flowers were deep purple. *They must change the flowers,* Connor thought.

"Why are we here?" Connor asked Liam.

"I gotta show you something. It's in my repository."

"Why not just pull it out of your box?" Connor asked.

"Hahaha, you think everything can fit in that tiny box? I can't shrink all of my things down.... Say, maybe that's your ability. You're kind of short. You shrink yourself?" he said playfully.

Connor gave him a friendly shove and countered, "You dumb nugget."

They laughed at themselves and ran towards the large wall. Liam verified his ornament and quickly pressed his code into the keypad. The Repository window popped open. He placed his arms in the box, and to Connor's surprise, he pulled out a brand new hot red hove bike.

"Wow! Where did you get that?!" Connor yelled.

"My father bought it for me before I left home. I was able to bring it. Should give it a try?"

"You bet! Are you rich? Those are supposed to be expensive," Connor questioned.

"We do ok," Liam smiled as he rested the bike on the floor.

"It's fantastic! Should we try it?!" Connor shouted.

"Wait, wait, wait, we can't ride it here. General Marks would throw us off the top of the Edifice. Follow me." Liam led the way. He dragged the floating bike behind him as Connor held the back frame to help him keep it steady.

They squeezed into the elevator. "Recreation," Liam spoke.

The black elevator doors opened to a coliseum-sized room. It was round, and the walls stretched taller than the tallest Sequoia tree. The room curved towards a bright hole in the roof. Connor looked on as a cyclical beam of light rested on a lush green field. He saw four rooms at each corner of the field. The field and rooms were surrounded by a large track that traced the outer edge of the room. There were operators in the field playing and a few older operators jogging around the track. "I've seen this place from up there," he said as he pointed to the hole in the roof.

Liam recalled as he looked up, "Yeh, that's Registration."

Connor noticed a breeze, and as he examined the walls, he could see tiny openings. They allowed a breeze to flow through this area of Eden to keep it cool.

"This is amazing," Connor said as he continued to look all around him. He heard a stinging crank and looked over at Liam on his bike. He quickly turned the right handle on the bar and called out, "Be right back!"

The bike hovered around the track in the opposite direction of the coming joggers. Two red robed operators quickly jumped out of the way to avoid the mobile mischief. Connor laughed and watched as Liam quickly made his way around the edge of the large coliseum. He lost sight of Liam for a moment but then saw him in the distance on the other side of the track past the field. A minute later he drove beside Connor and came to a halt.

"That couldn't get any better I'm afraid," Liam said as he crawled off. "Your turn, pal."

Connor excitedly mounted the bike and flew off down the track. He darted the opposite way that Liam traveled and couldn't go fast enough. He kept twisting the handle to push the bike faster and faster. He whizzed on but was quickly approaching four green robed operators strolling around the track. He shouted at them to signal his inevitable arrival, but no one looked back to see him. He traveled terribly close to their backs as they begin to look back in shock as if they were about to be assaulted.

"Look out!" he shouted. They scattered but hitting one of them seemed likely. Connor quickly tilted the bike and kept braking as he drifted towards the wall. Liam was jumping up and down in worry from across the way as he watched the stressful ride. As Connor drifted to the edge of the wall, he leaned over and kicked his foot on the ground giving the bike a nudge and moving its bottom side up the wall. He was sideways and driving on the wall when he felt his weight pulling him back down towards the track. He wittingly moved his body to try to angle the bike as he passed overhead of his terrified peers. The bike edged its way back along the ground and Connor felt more relaxed. Still, he began to lose concentration, and the bike weaved and wobbled. He tried to keep it steady as he applied pressure to the brakes and the bike jolted to a halt.

He crawled off the bike and waved back as to apologize to the others who barely escaped disaster.

He heard quick steps coming around the curve of the track.

"You nearly killed me... I almost died! What am I saying?! You nearly killed them! I... I... I'm sorry I don't mean to be so wound up," Liam shouted. He panted and tried to regain his breath from the quick sprint. "Maybe I should drive it back to the elevators."

"That's fine, I'm truly sorry. I didn't mean to do that."

"It's ok. To be honest, it was actually really awesome. How did you get up on the wall like that?" Liam questioned.

"I don't know… it just felt like the only thing I could do to get passed them," Connor replied.

"Well, I will probably never try it. I'm sure I would simply splatter on the track."

A red projection of General Marks appeared on the walls above them, and an amplified message followed.

"Connor Laurel and Liam Hudson, please report to the Registration room. Bring the hove bike but do not continue to use it," the voice of General Marks echoed. Feeling nervous and sheepish the boys walked back to the elevator with their heads hanging low.

"Registration," Connor moaned as the doors shut.

They arrived at the Registration room. Liam guided the bike out of the elevator and around the railing overlooking the field below. They spotted Mr. Templeton across the room reaching up high to grab a tool while he was balancing on a tiny chair. They kept walking forward and heard a loud crash behind them. They looked back and only saw two plump legs sticking high in the air as a mountain of gadgets poured and slipped down behind the desk. The boys paused to verify that Mr. Templeton was still alive. His feet wiggled, and he rolled around to emerge out of the clutter. The boys still feeling low smiled at one another and kept on.

They came to a large archway that read *Master Room*. A chrome door was sucked up into the ceiling showing them an open room. The room boasted two windows on each side that resembled the one in Dr. Finn's office. The outside sky appeared beautiful. They detected a shadow rotating on the clouds near them. It was the shadow of the Edifice above revolving slowly. Directly in front of them was a fancy and electronic desk that was dark gray but pulsated with tiny lights. A large and high chair sat behind the desk also gleaming. There were sofas and a few cushioned chairs surrounding a red rug untouched by dirt or dust. Behind them, as they trekked were two brilliant statues of the leaders of the Greater Coalition and the Minor Coalition.

Instantly the chrome door moved back down to the floor trapping them inside. Another door behind the tall chair opened into a dark corridor. In marched General Malinda Marks with sharp military garbs and a regal posture. She stopped after she passed through the door and took out a large keycard. She held it in front of a display near her doorway. The second chrome door came down as the display let out a modest *beep*.

The display was triangular. It did not resemble the ones the boy wore on their wrists.

"Sit down, boys," she commanded.

They sat on the sofa leaving the bike standing near the entrance. She walked around the chair and sat down in the towering seat behind the desk.

"I am General Melinda Marks. It is a pleasure to meet each of you in person. However, the nicety has been quite soured. It has come to my attention that each of you was involved in dangerous activities a few moments ago."

"It was my fault, General," Connor suggested.

"Do... Not... Speak..." She hissed. "I will only need hear you speak if I ask you a question first, Mr. Laurel."

Liam gulped.

"But I assure you, you do need to hear me... I will be taking that hove bike."

Liam wanted to beg for mercy but remained silent with a sad face.

"This is your first occurrence boys. It should have never been approved to bring the bike into Eden as it is. You see boys, it is my responsibility to make sure that we all remain safe. We are few in numbers, and we can't afford to injure one another because of mindless foolery. Each of you will remain in your bunks today during the Assembly. We'll be showing such a nice film. I do enjoy movies you know. This will be a lesson to each of you."

Connor was going to speak up but held his tongue only allowing a slight sound to escape. She opened her eyes wide, and with a sharp twitch, she presented a face that would threaten a lion.

"You... are each dismissed...."

The boys got up leaving the hove bike behind and started towards the opening front door.

"Don't let this happen again, boys," she said as the door closed behind them.

"You know what, Connor? I was wrong. What you did on the track wasn't scary at all. It was... was... exciting. But that," he pointed back to the office, "now that was scary."

"I agree, Liam. I'm sorry about the bike," he consoled.

He nodded back at Connor accepting the apology.

"Hi, boys!" they heard as Mr. Templeton was wobbling over.

"Hi, Mr. Templeton," Connor greeted and waved.

"Mr. Templeton, I don't know who it was... but they really did a number on that woman. They must have really broken her spirits. She's so... cold," Liam said shivering.

"Oh, General Marks?! She's just got an important job to do, my friend. You'll understand one day if you ever take on that much responsibility." He thought for an instant, "But, I suppose a nice wet kiss from a handsome man would soften her demeanor a bit." He laughed hardily as he pinched Connor's cheek suggesting that Connor could melt her heart.

"Ha-ha, I don't think so," Connor stated.

"See ya boys," Mr. Templeton walked on past them.

"Maybe we should get Dominic to give her a wet kiss," Connor suggested.

"I wouldn't wish that on anyone, pal. Not even that dimwit Dominic," Liam giggled at the thought.

"Reserves," Liam announced as they moved on.

The boys made their way back to the bunks and each reclined on their beds. They stared up at the ceiling to see a projection of water. It was as if they were resting on a sea floor. The sunshine danced through the water, and colorful fish swam over them. Connor mentioned, "Being under water is kind of scary, really."

"True... I just can't believe we got punished today. What happens if we get another occurrence? The year hasn't even properly started yet," Liam commented.

After some time, the ceiling announced. "Everyone make your way to the Assembly Hall. The movie will begin shortly." The boys jumped up and ran to the common room. They saw all of their peers rumbling with excitement towards the exit and moving down the halls.

"Come on boys what are you waiting for?" Natalie said as she trotted by.

"Didn't you hear? These degenerates tried to kill someone today in the Recreation Room," a familiar and annoying voice came from across the room. "I doubt they'll be able to leave the commons for a whole week," Dominic chuckled along with his posse.

"Do be quiet, Dominic," Natalie told him boldly.

"Fine then, if you love these criminals so much, stay here with them," he dared. "Or, you could come with us. We have great seats saved."

"I will stay here, actually," she countered.

Dominic was shocked that she was actually willing to skip the event. "Idiots," he muttered. Dominic signaled his crew along, and they headed towards the elevator.

"Dominic Eugene Knight. He makes Eden a little less extraordinary," Natalie commented. "What did you boys do?!" she exclaimed.

They explained the bike incident and discussed meeting the General.

"You would have cried at the sight of her. I felt so hopeless," Liam told her.

Natalie punched him on the shoulder with half her might and said, "I'm not that weak!"

Liam rubbed his arm and stepped away a bit.

"I'm gonna go get my tablet," Connor said as he started towards the bedroom. He opened the trunk, grabbed his tablet, and went back into the commons. Natalie and Liam were sitting on a comfy couch. Connor entered in and sat on a chair across from them as Liam explained how Mr. Templeton had fallen off the tiny chair earlier. Natalie laughed at his story.

Connor held his ornament up to his mouth. "Read Combative Training," he spoke.

A digital book of Combative Training showed up on the tablet's display.

"Are we really going to learn how to fight?" Connor asked the others.

"Yes, I think we'll learn the basics. My cousin says he didn't get decent until his second year here," Liam explained.

"Whoa..." Connor muttered as he flipped through the pages of the book.

"What?" Natalie asked.

"Look at this sword," Connor turned the tablet around and magnified the image for them. It was a long curved steel sword with one sharp edge. The handle was wrapped in black materials tightly, and it looked dangerous.

"Katana," Liam read out loud.

"It looks ancient, I've never seen one," Natalie added.

They were mesmerized over the thought of this image being learning material. Each of them continued to read through their books for school and talk for a few hours before they went to bed.

Class

Two days passed and it was the first day of classes. Connor woke up at 7:30 am as usual and got ready for the day. Roughly fifty brown and yellow robed children headed through the Rotunda towards the Analysis Hall. Connor was among the crowd. The group split in half as they entered two different classrooms.

Connor, Liam, Natalie, Dominic, and twenty-one others entered a classroom with desks facing a digital display in the front of the room. The desks were in elevated rows, and they were assorted around the room.

"Welcome to Physics!" a stylish man announced as he walked into the classroom towards the front of the room. He faced the students.

"I am Professor Benjamin Ozil." His name illuminated in fine cursive on the display behind him.

"Here we go," Connor breathed as he braced himself to endure the oncoming lecture.

The class lasted forty-five minutes, and their ornaments all buzzed in unison directing them to the next class. The students felt energized as they moved on to the next room over. The classroom was identical to the last one except this time when they entered, Dr. Finn was standing behind a floating table. There was an electronic globe spinning on the desk along with a spinning double helix made of plastic and a beautiful plant that was bright green and rustled a bit when students passed by.

"Hello, everyone. You all know me." He looked around to confirm he had met every child. "You have just embarked on an enchanting adventure," he paused with drama, "called Biology." He smiled and bowed.

Connor and Liam looked over to see Natalie with her face in her hand as she shook her head. They listened on as Dr. Finn lecture through facts and definitions. Once the class was over, they repeated the process two more times with two different professors. They wrapped up their morning classes and went down to the café for lunch.

"The sea bass and creamed toast smelled fantastic today," Natalie said as they entered the café.

They grabbed their trays and sat down at lavender colored table as oceanic themed music danced above.

"Liam, did you fall asleep during the trigonometry course?" Natalie asked.

"No. No. Of course not," he lied. "Eekk, this toast is cold," he placed his finger on the plate for a moment and the cream melted on his toast. "Anyone else?" he asked as he lifted his finger.

"Sure," Connor replied.

Liam held Connor's plate until the cream melted and spread onto the toast.

"No thanks," Natalie said. "I'm fine."

She held out her hand and formed three white napkins. They each grabbed one.

Once again Mr. Templeton vigorously waddled alongside the tables greeting operators as he went. He stopped at their table for a moment. He carried a tray so full of sea bass it could likely sink a boat.

"Oh, look who it is. The famous *troublemakers*," Mr. Templeton teased. "I hope you've been on your best behavior. You don't want the General after ya.... … … … YARR! YARR! YARR!" he barked towards Natalie startling her enough for her to fall off the bench. He let out the loudest and proudest laugh they had ever heard as Natalie slithered back up to the table, straightened her robe, and fixed her hair.

"Very amusing, sir," she muttered.

He smiled and patted her on the back to assure her he meant no harm. The boys heard a stiff march behind him as they caught a glimpse of the General speaking and listening into her ornament in a very attentive manner.

"I'd love to know what she's saying. You don't think it's about us do you?!" Liam cowered.

Connor winced at the idea.

"Now see here, Mr. Hudson. It's not right to listen in on people's private conversations. It's unethical really. That's why I program each and every ornament to be completely safe of spying. If someone wants to record a message it has to be their voice and their command only," he explained. Mr. Templeton stood proudly and just before the children after his speech. "Good day," he said as he went on down the row laughing and greeting others.

"I dare say that you struck a nerve, Liam," Natalie said sarcastically.

"I believe so, I didn't realize it was such a big deal to him. I thought these devices recorded everything we said regardless of our commands or voices," Liam replied.

"Curious," Connor whispered as he viewed his ornament. It pulsated with a dim shine. The tabletop changed to baby blue as they got up and went on to their next class.

They marched up to a large open classroom with their tablets in hand. The floor was large, and a black padded mat covered most of the area. The front of the room was covered with mirrors. They saw an empty shelf on the wall adjacent with the doorway. They huddled around along the wall waiting for the class to start. Colonel Albert entered the room, but instead of his usual clothing, he wore tight crimson robes.

"Place your tablet on the shelf, remove your shoes, and line up on the matt," he sounded off.

The children hesitated and looked at one another.

"NOW!" he shouted.

They scrambled and crawled over one another to hurry and get into place. The children aligned two rows facing him as he had his back to the mirror. One scrawny child tripped on the edge of the mat and quickly recovered to jump in line. The colonel sneered at the young operator for a moment.

"This is Combative Training. I will be teaching you how to defend yourself. The use of Impetus in this class will be prohibited.

"Rubbish," Dominic said lowly.

"Dominic Knight!!! One more negative comment and I will throw you from this classroom myself!" the Colonel shouted with meaning.

"Your Impetus is not your defense. It is not a weapon. They are an addition to your being, and they will not save you if you are threatened. Discipline, knowledge, control, and balance are your defenses."

Connor clung to every word the Colonel was saying.

"If your mind can endure, then so will your body," he finished. "Now, I need five volunteers." No one moved. "I won't hurt you, I promise." No one moved. He pointed to five random students. Liam was one of them. He directed them to stand a few feet away surrounding him.

"I want each of you to attack me as if your life depended on it. If you fail to do so, I will send you straight to the Master room, and you can sit with the General for the remainder of the day. I'm sure Mr. Laurel and Mr. Hudson have told you about their pleasant time with her," he said as he looked at Connor.

Connor looked down with a hint of shame.

"Ok, attack me…now!"

The children attacked him all at the same time. He blocked a punch towards his abdomen and sat the student down before he could finish striking. Meanwhile, the colonel lifted his back leg to intercept a kick and pushed another student backward towards her classmates. He then stepped back and received simultaneous arms reaching to strike his upper body. He spun them around as if he were dancing with them. They each locked arms and he sat them down with light force. Finally, Liam came screeching from behind to tackle him, but the instructor bent down as Liam flipped over his body through the air. The Colonel reached out to help him land softly.

The class clapped for the terrific performance as the five students sat defeated.

"Stop clapping," he said. They all stood straight as arrows and regained their serious posture. The Colonel explained, "You just witnessed two portions of the combative skill. First, the knowledge to defend myself from my attackers. Secondly, you observed control to defend without injuring my attackers. If you can obtain these principles in this class, then you will be a fierce opponent in any situation."

Connor understood and soaked up every word. This class was the most interesting to him because for the first time he felt even with his peers. No one could use their abilities, and that comforted Connor since he had not found his Impetus. For the remainder of the class, the students practiced form with basic blocks and defensive techniques.

Connor moved along to the Group Based Tactics class where he learned military terms and completed physical challenges paired in small groups.

It was time for the final class of the day. Their ornaments lead them out of the Analysis Hall and into the Rotunda. Connor was uncertain where they were going. All of his classes and tests had been held in the Analysis corridor. They moved past the Infirmary and onto an escalator. They then walked up a second escalator.

Connor and the students walked along through a round opening. The area inside was shaped like a sphere. On the floor was an indention leading to six large capsules. There was a railing around the indention and a few steps that led down to the capsules level. There was stadium seating around the capsules and a large cubed display hung above them.

A message scrolled on each side of the hanging cube. *Aviation, Simulation, and Strategies.* A single light shined on the opposite end of the entrance over a man standing on a platform with a screen behind him.

"Please do have a seat wherever you'd like," he announced. The children sat in random seats of the spherical room. The students noticed as the rest of the fifty or more brown and yellow robes bustled in.

The man wore a blue cap with golden stitched eagles on the front. He wore a blue suit to match and presented a ceremonial golden rope on his shoulder. He had dark tawny eyes. Gray hair was shoved into the cap with a small layer of thickness around the lining.

"I am Captain Doyen Brookmeyer. I have been away from Eden for quite some time and have accepted the call to aid the teaching of aviation…" he introduced. He had a scruffy voice and rugged presence.

"Man has traveled to different planets with ease, our modern technology in the air is smarter than ever before, and our weaponry has become quite efficient. Still, time proves over and over again the need for human control for a successful flight. Artificial intelligence is helpful, but you my fellow operators, you're better."

Connor noticed Dominic smiling arrogantly a couple of seats over.

"These six capsules will simulate every necessary situation to get you prepared for basic flight maneuvers. I, and the rest of the class will be able to watch and study your movements on the screens above."

Connor was ecstatic. He loved flying. Even the small lift off from Liam's hove bike brought him joy. The captain continued to lecture for the remainder of the class. Connor's ornaments began to buzz, and the students started back to their quarters to enjoy the rest of the evening.

"You guys go ahead," Connor told the Liam and Natalie.

Connor recognized the capsules on the ground level. These were a much better version of the one he wanted to try out in the museum back home. The captain was on the ground level checking the capsules and writing onto his tablet.

"Sir, may I look inside?" Connor asked with bravery.

"Oh, sure, let me show you." The captain opened one of the hatches and showed him the inside. "Here is the throttle… you'll use this to communicate with your teammates," he pointed to different devices. "These will fire your available armaments, and these monitors will show your cabin pressure, altitude, etc."

Connor felt like he was looking into an alien space ship. To him, it was. This technology seemed to surpass his expectations, and he was very intrigued. *I wish dad could see this!* he thought trying not to dance in excitement.

"You'll learn much more than that I assure you. I must be going though," the Captain concluded. Connor smiled and wanted to give the man a hug. However, he refrained and only knew to salute him. The captain grinned, stood at attention, and saluted back. Connor turned and went after his friends to tell them what he had examined.

Connor caught up with his friends in the common room. He began to chat with Liam, Natalie, and a few others. He told them all about the capsules, and they tried to guess when they would use them.

"The captain seemed nice," Connor mentioned.

"Yes, I thought his introduction was curious though. I wonder when he trained here. I wonder where he's been," Natalie added.

"He's the military type, I imagine he served in the Greater Coalition Air Force," Liam commented.

"I suppose," Connor concluded.

An operator walked into the room, "Hey, did you hear?! Marcella Prevost found her Impetus!" he shouted. The group in the room emptied to see the new operator. Connor looked over to Liam and Natalie, and they shot up to join the group.

They entered into another common room packed full of yellow and green robed operators trying to view her in the middle of the room. Connor and his companions couldn't see over the crowd. Liam looked at Natalie, "Make a stool or ladder or something!"

"Are you crazy?! That would take an eternity, and I can't concentrate with all of these people being loud," she said.

Connor swiped a chair and shoved it over to the corner of the room. "Come on!" he shouted. They all balanced on the chair the best they could.

The crowd chanted, "Do It! Do it! Do it!" as they were excited to see what would happen. Marcella looked around the crowd nervously. She stood still and closed her eyes tight. The tiny girl held her arms out wide, and her body seemed to stretch apart. One operator in the crowd moaned, "Ewww!!!" As she stretched, her body started to separate and before them stood two Marcellas. The crowd clapped, and they all celebrated the achievement.

"Wow," Connor whispered.

Each Marcella spun in a circle and bumped into each other becoming one Marcella again. Someone passed a yellow robe over the heads of the onlookers. She held the yellow robes high showing her prize to the mob. Connor, Liam, and Natalie made their way back to their wing of the Reserves. They said goodnight and got ready for bed.

Clock

Two weeks passed, and business continued as usual. Connor was settling into his studies, and he was comfortable with the day to day activities. He sat in his room by himself reading his tablet. He was reading his Physics book to prepare for a test. While reading a complicated formula, his wrist vibrated. His ornament displayed that he had received a message. He spoke, "Play message."

"Connor! Come to my father's office! Quick!" Natalie's voice played. She seemed happy.

Connor finished reading a bit, placed his tablet in his bedside chest, and was on his way to the Analysis Hall. He walked through the Rotunda and felt a quick ache to his lower back. He reached behind him as he walked to feel the area. "Ouch..." he thought for a moment. As he entered the corridor, the pain subsided. "I guess I was sitting on my bed too long."

He arrived in front of Dr. Finn's office, but there was an eerie quiet in the halls. He hadn't passed by anyone on the way, and the room was very dark. He took small safe steps and announced, "Um... hello??"

The window shade flew open to let light in and a group of students shouted, "Surprise!"

Stunned, he stepped back and lost his footing. He fell to the ground and laid there for a moment laughing at himself.

"Happy Birthday, friend," Liam said as he reached down to pick him up. Connor stretched his torso and reached down and touched his toes to stretch his back.

"Thanks, guys!"

The office was lightly decorated, and a two-tiered strawberry cake sat on Dr. Finn's desk. Natalie and a handful of yellow robed operators were there for the cake. Connor noticed Dr. Finn in the corner of the room enjoying the show. Dr. Finn walked over to his conveyor belt and started grabbing drinks as they appeared. He passed them around to the students.

"Connor, I'm so glad you're here," Dr. Finn went on, "The thirteenth year is arguably the most important year of an operator's life. It's when everything changes." Connor smiled as he watched Natalie light the candles with a tiny white torch. "Well, go ahead Connor," Dr. Finn said.

Connor thought about the last time he saw his parents. They baked him a simple cake the day he left. This day was supposed to be the day he and his parents would go to the museum and visit the ice cream shop. He felt his eyes water as he took a deep breath. He knew he would speak to his parents soon, but he felt that his life at Eden had meaning. He didn't have a special ability or power, but he knew he was right where he was supposed to be. That was a peaceful thought.

"Make a wish," Natalie suggested with a sweet smile.

At that moment, he began to push air through his lips. He could have wished to be back with his parents. He could have wished to be home in his room again. He could have wished to return to the normal life. Instead, he wished that his Impetus would be revealed. Connor had matured. He blew out the candles and the room filled with applause. The group started eating and drinking and enjoying the free afternoon.

The party came to a close, and the others began to move on. "Come on, Connor. We're going to Recreation Room," Liam proposed.

He looked back and watched Dr. Finn create a bag out of thin air. The doctor started to put empty cups and plates into the bag. "Go on ahead. I'll catch up," Connor responded. "I'll help you, Doctor."

"Oh, Connor, that is a nice gesture, but I'm almost done. I'm glad you stayed back though. I wanted to catch up," he said as he continued to drop dishes in the bag.

"Sounds good," Connor said.

"So how are you enjoying your classes? I'm sure biology is your favorite!" he said jokingly.

"Biology isn't bad, sir. I've learned plenty. If I'm quite honest, I would say that Combative Training and Aviation are my favorites."

Dr. Finn responded, "I can't say I blame you. When I was your age, I preferred afternoon classes. It wasn't until two years later that I really became quite interested in the sciences. That's when I decided I would one day study at a university."

"It sounds… as if things are the same around here… like they were back then," Connor replied.

"Oh, nothing has changed. The professors and some of the staff have changed but overall, it's the same. It's a good though. We've saved many lives and protected many identities." Dr. Finn continued, "My daughter seems to like you and Mr. Hudson. She needs good friends. I appreciate you being kind to her."

"No problem, she really has been a great friend," Connor said.

"Have you had any feelings or any hints to your ability yet, Connor?" he asked as he tied up the bag and placed it on the conveyor belt. The belt began to move, and the bag was taken away. They each sat down and continued to talk as they looked at the pink sky rippling from the sun behind the horizon.

"No, unfortunately I haven't a clue, sir."

"Now that you're thirteen, we'll start to scan you more like other brown robed children," Dr. Finn explained.

"But, Dr. Finn, I have classes all day."

"Yes," he interrupted. "You'll be sleeping in one of our testing rooms until your Impetus is revealed. It's standard procedure, so you won't be alone. We can scan you as you sleep since you'll be busy during the day."

Connor was comforted. "How many more brown robed children are left, sir?"

"Five, including you… you're the last one to turn thirteen. It usually doesn't take long for us to pinpoint it and help you along. My wife was the same way," he added.

"Your wife had an Impetus?" Connor asked.

"Yes, she did… I met her here. She was one of the few in our group that took a while to find her Impetus. It wasn't until she was scanned that she became aware of what her power could be," he explained. He stared in a trance admiring the beauty of the pink sky.

"She could change the color of anything you see. I would come home after a long day, and my Felicity would make our family room a brand new color to match my mood. She always knew what I was feeling. She would paint beautiful pictures by simply watching a blank surface or page. I remember making a clock. It took me a few hours to get the gears and machinery working right. Once it appeared, I hung it on the wall. She was so proud. She lifted her hand, and the color of the clock changed into a beautiful shade of green… my favorite color."

Connor felt sorry for the Doctor. "She sounded terrific, sir. Felicity Finn."

"Yes, that was her name. I wish Natalie would have known her. She passed away when Natalie was born. They really are so similar. Oh, my... look at the time. I'm going on and on," he said as he stopped staring at the sunset. "You run along, if you ever need anything you can come to me, Connor. I'm here for you." He reached out and patted young Connor on the shoulder.

Connor started down the hallway. He made his way down to the Recreation room to walk and talk with his friends before dinner time.

Days passed and the time came when Connor would finally get to speak to his parents. It was an off day, and Connor was being directed by his ornament to head to the Rotunda. As he was walking down the hall, Liam and Natalie came running behind him. They ran straight ahead, and Liam looked back not even realizing he'd just flown by Connor.

Connor was confused. Liam and Natalie were not wearing their robes. They were wearing something else entirely. Liam and Natalie wore tight, modest rubbery suits. They were bright yellow and covered them from the top of their arms down to the top of their knees. On their torsos were designs. Natalie had the design of a dolphin and Liam had the design of a bear.

"Where's your swimwear?" Liam asked.

"Swimwear?"

"Yeh, didn't you see the announcement. It's Beach day. The summer's about to end ya know," Liam continued.

"There's a beach?"

"Yeh," Liam said.

"In Eden?"

Liam went on, "Yeh! Well, no, not a real beach. They make the Recreation Room into a beach."

"Oh, I must have missed the announcement. I'm going to talk to my parents," Connor explained.

Natalie walked over and put her hand on his shoulder and gave an enduring smile. Connor gave her a look of confidence as he patted her hand on his shoulder.

"Well, your suit should be in your box when you're done. We'll see you down there." They scurried on.

Once Connor reached the Rotunda, he was directed to go up an escalator. He tried to sort out in his mind how there could be a beach in the Recreation Room. The green arrow on his ornament pointed left after he climbed the first escalator. As he kept on, he walked passed Marcella in her new yellow robes hurrying past him. "Hi, Connor!" she said.

"Hi," he replied. His ornament halted him by a chrome door further down. A display next to the door projected an image of Professor Ozil.

"Come in, come in, Connor," the image spoke invitingly.

The chrome door went up revealing another black door. The black door opened away from Connor revealing yet another door. The final door was also chrome, and it started to ease down and back like a draw bridge. The final door became a wide bridge leading to a large square room. Connor walked across the bridge carefully. When he looked over the edge of the bridge, he couldn't see a bottom. It was a dark abyss. He kept his eyes forward to make sure he got across as quickly as possible.

He entered a square room that was completely white. In the middle of the room were a seat and a display that was connected to the floor at its bottom. Connor noticed a window in the room and on the other side was Professor Ozil.

"I'm sorry about the scary bridge, Mr. Laurel. You have entered the Secure Room. This is where you will communicate with your family. Take a seat, and I'll explain," he directed.

Connor could only see the professor through the clear window within a blank gray room.

Professor Ozil explained, "Your parents have received a tablet and an exact time for when they can speak to you. You will be speaking to them in five minutes. You'll have around ten minutes to talk, and unfortunately, we'll have to cut the transmission. Most of our students understand why we can't reveal our activities here so this shouldn't be hard for you. Remember, you are in a medical facility, and you are being tested and provided for. Do keep any *advanced* details to yourself."

"The transmission between you and your parents will be a bit delayed. This is to make sure that if you do slip up and say something suspicious, we can edit it. We do not want to worry your parents after all. If you do say something inappropriate, you will see this." He pointed. The wall behind the display faintly sparkled red.

"Your parents will simply see a garbled video and audio feed and will assume that there is interference. Having said that, the more you focus on what you're saying, the more time you'll have to speak with them without any interference. It's almost time now. Any questions?" the professor asked as he looked down at his ornament.

Connor thought for a moment. "Um... no.... I suppose not."

"Great. Your parents will arrive on the screen within the next three minutes. I'm sure you'll be splendid," the professor said positively.

Connor sat quietly staring at a blank screen. He was nervous. He worried about his parents. He worried that they were sad about him being gone. He didn't know what to expect from the call. The room dimmed a bit, and his parents appeared on screen. They were sitting close together at the kitchen table. He recognized the cabinets from home in the background. His mother covered her mouth and smiled.

"Hey, sport!" Timothy spoke, "How are you, do you feel ok?"

"We miss you!" Sybil shouted as she lowered her hand.

"I'm great! I have made a couple of friends," Connor replied.

"That's wonderful, sweetie," his mother said lovingly.

"I feel fine; they've just been scanning me, it's painless though." Connor continued, "I'm just waiting to get my abil.... ab...." He froze.

The wall behind the display sparkled red.

"What's that son? Are you there?!" his father asked. "This stupid thing," Timothy looked as if he was slapping the side of the display.

"I'm here!" Connor recovered.

"Oh, ok we see you now," his mom mentioned.

"It's really not bad here. The food is tasty, and I'm doing schoolwork, so I won't be behind when I come home," Connor assured them.

"That is so great, sport!" his father replied.

They went on to speak for a few more minutes. Connor's father received a raise at the factory, and his mother told him to be expecting a gift.

"I love you, both," Connor said as they concluded.

His mother responded, "We'll see you again soon. Stay strong."

"We love you," Timothy finished.

The screen went dark, and the familiar feeling of anguish filled Connor's stomach.

"That was impressive, Mr. Laurel! Only one slip up," Professor Ozil assured him. "Now, run along! It's Beach day!"

Connor stood up and sighed lightly. The doors behind him opened again, and he passed over the bridge and back into the Rotunda. He started on his way as he passed by a boy headed for the Secure Room.

"Hey, I know you," Connor said.

It was the boy who had arrived in the landing bay with him weeks ago.

He let out an apprehensive, "Hi."

"You're in the aviation class right?" Connor asked.

"Yes. I am," he said shyly.

"Connor Laurel, nice to meet you."

"Oh… I... I'm... Phillip... Donaghue," the boy stuttered. He still wore brown robes just like Connor.

"Pleasure," Connor said, "It's not bad in there. Professor Ozil will walk you through it."

They shook hands and were each on their way.

Connor arrived near his bed and saw his chest wave a white glow across the top. He unlocked the box and looked inside. He pulled out a rubber suit like Natalie and Liam's except it was a brown. He held it in front of him, and he saw a white logo on the front of a fierce dragon. He placed it on the bed and caught sight of his night light and manual resting at the bottom of the box. Feeling sentimental, he pulled each out and gave them a slight grasp as to hug them.

"You really are creepy," he heard as he saw Dominic pass by through the doorway wearing swimwear.

Connor quickly relaxed his arms and murmured, "Jerk...."

He put the objects back in the box, changed into his swimwear, and went down to the recreation room.

As the black elevator doors opened into the recreation room, he was dumbfounded. Instead of a track in front of him, there was a large amount of sand. There was a wavy ocean where the field used to reside, and the walls were blue and projected a bright sun. The wall looked as if there were boats in the distance. The water seemed to go on forever in a distant horizon. Connor caught a glimpse of Liam and Natalie among the hundreds of operators. He sprinted towards them but struggled through the deep sand. The air was cool and salty.

"Hi, Connor!" Natalie greeted him.

"How is this possible?" he asked.

"Well, from what I can see, the pool ends where the wall usually does. The projections are very convincing though. We can't swim very far out," Liam said as he drip dried in the artificial sun.

Connor without hesitation ran and jumped into the imitation ocean. It tasted salty as some of the liquid found its way into his mouth. He swam under and then splashed above the water. He spat out the excess water and chuckled to himself. He could feel waves pushing against his body but wasn't quite sure how it was happening.

He swam back to the shore after enjoying the scene for a while. He marched through warm sand and back to Natalie and Liam's spot on the beach. They were talking with cups in hand. The drinks were full of tiny ice particles and had a purple hue.

"Hey, Connor! Catch!" Natalie exclaimed as she held her hand up towards him.

He was dripping wet and looked at her with confused eyes. Suddenly, a large inflated red and white striped ball fell on his head.

"Whoa! Nice!" Liam said as he laughed at the sight of this ball landing on Connor's head.

She had formed a beach ball out of thin air a few feet above him. The hit to the head was soft and playful. Connor laughed and kicked the ball over to another group of operators. The ball continued to bounce to-and-fro around the beach as Connor, Natalie, and Liam had the most fun since they'd arrived.

Note

"Ahhh... Hmph... Yuuuah..." Connor exhaled as he blocked two quick punches and a kick.

He punched back. He quickly jabbed twice with his right arm while holding his left fist up near his chin. He bent slightly and kicked with his right leg. Natalie blocked each strike with confidence. Connor took a step back and they each bowed to one another as sweat dripped from their hair and face.

"Very good. Exemplary form, Ms. Finn, and good concentration Mr. Laurel," colonel Albert complimented them as he stood behind the rest of the students in the class. "Return to the mat, each of you."

"Who's next?" the colonel announced.

Connor and Natalie plopped on the mat as two other students went to the front of the room to spar.

"You didn't have to go easy on me," Natalie whispered.

"I... I wasn't," Connor replied feeling a bit deflated.

"I could take you both myself," Liam whispered loudly from behind.

"Quiet please!" the Colonel shouted as the two other students began to exchange blows.

Connor watched as students practiced the blocks and basic strikes they learned over the past two months.

"That was a good session. Try to relax. Some of you are still a bit stiff. We'll start escaping holds next time. You're dismissed," the colonel instructed.

The group exited the room and entered the hallway.

"I wish we had time to shower before aviation," Natalie commented.

"I do too. You reek!" Liam joked.

"Oh. Ha! Ha! Ha!" she laughed sarcastically.

"The robe does feel sticky," Connor added.

They walked further down the hall and into the Rotunda.

"Is it Halloween already?" Liam asked.

Natalie corrected him, "No, silly; it's not for another two weeks."

"Are you sure? Because I think I spot a monster," he said lowly as he tried to avoid attention.

Connor looked across the room and witnessed General Marks walking towards them through the large domed space.

"Mr. Laurel!" she said firmly. "I will need you to follow me." She gave a cold stare at Natalie and Liam. Slightly frightened, they left Connor to his own devices with the intimidating lady.

"Come along," she said.

They walked back into the Analysis Hall passing by combative training class. She stopped at a familiar room. She commanded, "Go in." Connor walked into scanning Room 22. "Your new rounds of scans will start tonight. You will come here to sleep from now until you are instructed otherwise. Is that clear?"

"Yes, ma'am," he responded.

"Good. Your chest is there," she pointed to the corner of the room.

The room was small and only housed reclined seat. *At least I get my box,* he thought.

"Any questions?" she asked.

"No... no ma'am."

She looked at him coldly and headed back into the Rotunda. His arm started to vibrate. Connor looked down at his ornament's display. Aviation class had started. "Agh. I'm late." He rushed into the Rotunda and dashed up the escalators. He arrived in the large round entry way, and the Captain stopped lecturing.

"Better late than never. Don't let it happen again," the Captain pronounced.

Connor assured him, "No sir, it won't."

Dominic who was seated near him looked back at two other operators and murmured, "Typical." They snickered quietly. Connor sat in the closest empty seat he could find.

"Being late can be problematic. Being early can be equally problematic when you're in the air. As we have covered, most of the aircraft systems give us the ability to land by hovering and stopping over a safe location. However, I would be doing you all a disservice if we did not practice landing in emergency situations. Every aircraft today has a backup mechanism so that we can land as we fly at a slower speed onto a runway. Mr. Donaghue, will you join me on the floor please?"

Philip stood up sheepishly and made his way down to the capsules. Captain Brookmeyer opened the casing of the front capsule and beckoned Philip to enter. Philip rolled into the cockpit, and the captain closed him inside.

He galloped back up to his podium and display. He spoke to the class and Philip. "Ok, I'm going to start you in the air. Your primary landing systems will not work. We covered this in the last lecture... I hope you all were listening."

Connor looked up to see the cubed display showing Philip inside for all of the class to see. The class could see his view within the simulation, his hands, and his face. The lights dimmed, and Philip's capsule began to shimmer from the outside. The class could see exactly what Philip was experiencing.

"Head for the landing strip, Mr. Donaghue," the Captain commanded.

Phillip looked to his right, and he saw a landing strip in the distance. The terrain around it was a jungle, and the runway had a dark top with beige lines. Connor thought to himself and knew every procedure perfectly. He never missed a word of the captain's lectures. The simulated aircraft turned on its side and aligned with the runway.

"Good, Phillip, 2000 feet and descending."

Connor watched as Phillip began to pull back on the throttle and tried to steady his craft. He pressed three green buttons and flipped a switch. The secondary landing system engaged and tiny wheels appeared on the bottom of the craft. He reduced speed, and his wheels scratched the surface making a screeching noise. The craft bounced and landed again. It rolled on at a great speed. Phillip leaned his head back with a sigh of relief.

"Very good, Mr. Donaghue. You landed your craft and almost lived," the Captain announced.

"What?!" Philip shouted. Phillip grabbed the control stick as the capsule rattled on the inside. His aircraft rolled off the runway and into a thick area of trees. The craft broke apart and started burning in flames. Philip screamed dramatically as he was truly scared.

The Captain explained, "You forgot to use the brake."

"Come now boy, don't wet your pants in there." The capsule popped open, and Philip scurried back to his seat.

"It requires the greatest of attention to achieve perfect landing as you just witnessed. I want all of you to write an essay explaining the differences of landing a transport craft and a fighter craft. It will be due next week," he instructed.

The class let out low groan, and the captain continued to lecture for the remainder of the session.

That night, Connor walked to Room 22 to his new bedroom. He got inside and laid back on the reclining chair as the door latched. Just like before, a light showed above him that resembled moonlight.

"Dragon," he whispered into his ornament.

The dragon flew into sight and landed on the surface of his display. It shook and flapped its wings fiercely causing his ornament to vibrate a bit. He placed his finger on the dragon and rubbed its wings. The dragon screeched and blew fire.

"Yo-yo," Connor whispered. The dragon launched into the air and made a loop back towards the surface. "Blaze." The dragon stepped back and breathed an intense stream of flames four feet above Connor's display. "Good boy," Connor whispered as he stroked the dragon on the head.

The dragon disappeared, and the ornament read, "New message."

"Play," Connor stated.

Liam's voice spoke, "Hey, pal. I grabbed an extra sugar biscuit from the café'. But... I'm not hungry." The message stopped playing. Connor saw a flash in the corner of his eye. He stepped over to his box and opened it. Inside was a slightly dried sugar biscuit that was missing part of its round edge.

"He took a bite." Connor chuckled to himself. He held his ornament close to his mouth.

"Record message for Liam Hudson," he said as he paused for a moment.

"Thanks. I was feeling a bit hungry actually."

"Send."

He walked back over to the chair and nibbled on the biscuit and then fell soundly to sleep.

After several nights of sleeping alone, Connor began to worry. "I'll never find my Impetus. There's been a mistake in the system." He thought that any day General Marks would find him, throw him in a hove rover, and send him back home. He shivered at the thought of leaving his new life. The food, the friends, the games, the studies, everything was better than back home.

He imagined living in Eden permanently. He would live there with his mom and dad until he was ready to attend a University. "What about Samantha?" he pondered. He thought about how much she would love this miraculous place. He missed her and did not want to admit it.

It was an off day, and he stepped into the Analysis Hall exiting Room 22. He saw Dr. Finn down the hall and gave him a quick wave. Dr. Finn waved back and went on towards his office. The door to Room 24 opened across the hall and Philip walked out. "Will we ever be like the others?" Philip asked in a mopey manner.

"I'm not sure, Philip... I'm just not sure. At least we have each other, right?" he said as he tugged on his brown robe. He was trying to encourage Philip.

"Yeh. That's true."

"Hey, Philip. I'm going down to References with Liam and Natalie to study for the sociology exam. You should come along," Connor invited.

"Really?" Philip said with excitement.

"Sure, but... don't forget your tablet."

"Definitely." Philip went back in the Room 24 and came back with his tablet. They walked to the elevator and Philip spoke, "References." The two boys arrived at the room of electronic hardware towers and joined the others at a table.

"I know it's a bit warmer here, but it's easier to study. It can get loud in the common rooms," Liam said. They sat viewing their tablets and reading over their notes. Connor's ornament vibrated. He held it up to check it.

A smooth woman's voice read aloud,

"*Your current grades are.... Sociology - A.... Trigonometry - C...*

Biology - B.... Physics - B...."

The recording stopped.

"C???" Natalie fretted. "You have a C, Connor?!"

"It's ok, friend... I have a C in that class as well," Liam consoled him.

"What?! That's preposterous!" Natalie raised her voice.

"What? That's average," Liam replied.

Connor agreed, "Yeh."

"Boys! You need to study more. You're both above average!" she scolded them.

The woman's voice sounded off again but this time across the table.

"Your current grades are...

Sociology - A.... Trigonometry - A...

Biology - A.... Physics - A..."

Philip sat his ornament back down by his side and smugly smiled at all of them. They looked at one another in astonishment.

"I almost forgot. A girl from the common rooms asked me to come and watch her perform today. I was hoping you two would join me. Oh, and you too, of course," Natalie said as she gestured to Philip.

"I'd be delighted," Philip responded.

"Meh... I suppose," Liam moaned. Natalie gave him a sideways look of disappointment.

"It'll be great I'm sure," Connor piped up trying to reinforce Natalie. They continued to study for another hour or so and made their way to the Recreation room.

They entered the room, and it had the same field and four buildings along the corners. The track was populated with operators, and the ceiling seemed festive with scarlet, mustard, and apricot tints. They walked to the second building on the far corner of the field and walked up a small flight of stairs to a doorway. On their way to the room, the coliseum projected leaves falling from time to time as low as their feet.

They entered the room to a row of chairs facing a small stage. A girl with an ocean blue robe and long curly tangerine hair stood with a flute to her lips. She played a happy melody and swayed from side to side. The four of them sat down in empty seats and noticed a few other operators listening to her song. She held a long note and ended. The room gave a courteous applause, and she began again. The tune was sweet, had a smooth rhythm, and was in the key of A minor. Connor looked next to him to see Philip entranced by the music.

She ended her second song a few minutes later and took a bow. She pressed a display behind her, and a tray lowered to the stage. She placed the flute on its surface, and it retracted back into the ceiling.

"That was simply beautiful," Natalie said as she stepped off the stage.

"Right on!" Philip announced awkwardly.

"Thank you very much," the girl responded. They continued to chat for a moment and returned to the beautiful coliseum.

The children continued to attend classes day in and day out. Connor slept alone in Room 22 night after night. It was getting close to the winter break, and Connor continued to grow anxious of the thought that he may not be an operator. Only two people with brown robes remained. Connor and Philip.

"Dr. Finn, I just don't understand! Have the systems gotten any clues yet?" Connor asked with aggravation. He was visiting Dr. Finn in his office. He had a small wired tree in the corner of the room with a dark green star on top. It cycled through dim amber, and cream lights and dark green bulbs hung from the branches. A few wrapped gifts sat underneath. Dr. Finn was looking out of his office window while sipping hot mint chocolate through a clear mug. The window was frosted, and he wore a dark coat.

"I understand your frustration, Connor. I truly do. The General hasn't mentioned any clues to me," he replied.

"Maybe she hates me."

"My dear boy, I assure you she doesn't hate you. And besides finding your Impetus is entirely out of her control."

"I suppose," Connor groaned.

"Connor, the winter break is two weeks long. It's a chance for you to go back home and spend time with your family. However, you won't be leaving until the second week."

"What?! Why?" Connor asked.

"Most people have found their Impetus by this time of year. We aren't getting any leads through your scans. We're going to scan you more that week to try to collect more data. I will be here and so will Natalie. You won't be completely alone. Natalie won't be visiting her aunt until the second week," he mentioned. "Correct me if I'm wrong but, Philip Donahue still hasn't found his Impetus either... Correct?"

"No sir, he hasn't. We're both worried," Connor said.

"I'm sure you are, and that's completely natural," the doctor comforted Connor as he handed him a mug of freshly made hot mint chocolate.

"Sometimes it just takes a moment... a moment of clarity to realize your Impetus. Some operators say their Impetus came along when they saw, heard, smelled, felt, or even tasted something. Like my Felicity, I remember as if it were yesterday. Her Impetus seemed delayed just like yours. We were sitting in the Repository admiring the plants and the river. While we were there, the flowers started to change colors, and I pointed it out. She sat there... staring. I thought she was getting sick or maybe going mad. But then, suddenly she lifted her hand, and she changed a single flower petal to a beautiful violet shade."

"That sounds lovely, sir," Connor said.

"It was... It truly was, Connor. Why don't you go down to the Recreation room and take a walk? The decorations are inspiring this time of year. I would not be surprised if your Impetus found you before the holiday," he encouraged him with a fatherly smile.

"Ok sir, I will. Thanks for the mint chocolate," Connor said graciously.

"Don't mention it. Now you go ahead," Dr. Finn signaled him forward.

Connor went along feeling invigorated from the excellent hot mint chocolate. He came across Liam and Natalie in the Rotunda. They were walking towards the Assembly Hall.

"Hey, you two, where are you going?" Connor asked.

"We were going to see if the Assembly hall had been decorated yet," Natalie replied.

"Oh, I wouldn't know, I just talked to your Father. He did mention the Recreation room being decorated though," Connor said.

"Really?!" Natalie shouted, "let's go!"

"Alright," Liam and Connor agreed simultaneously.

"Recreation," Natalie shouted with excitement as the elevator doors closed in front of them.

The doors opened to an amazing sight. The walls projected a rural village glowing and covered in white snow. The room was projecting snowflakes all around them. On the ground, they stepped on layers of soft ice. In the middle of the field stood a large tree with ropes glowing red. Golden cubes were hanging from the branches glistening continuously. The top boasted a large red star with each point twinkling. The star was nearly tall enough to reach the Registration Room above. They began to walk around the track. The sound of warm horns and spirited strings played jolly music throughout the coliseum. As they stamped through the cold snow, they noticed a snowball fight breaking out. Dominic was the instigator and looked as if he was trying to inflict pain. The group seemed playful as the battle carried on.

Connor looked at Natalie and spoke, "I was talking to your father, Natalie. He said that Impetus comes to people sometimes when they experience something."

"I had almost forgotten you didn't have yours yet," she said. "I suppose he's right. I received my gift when I was back at my aunt's house. I was searching for a thread to repair a rip in my favorite bag. I searched and searched and searched, and as I was hunting... I stood there for a moment and felt energy come over me. I looked on a side table in my aunt's bedroom, and that's when a tiny needle appeared."

"That's amazing," Connor said. He wished that he could create a needle, or thread, or anything for that matter. "I'm going to walk over to the tree. I just need a minute to think."

"Sure thing, friend," Liam replied.

Connor began to walk, and as he got closer, he began to marvel at the tree in the middle. He noticed snow all over the field, and the four buildings had been decorated to match the projections on the wall. He kept walking forward, and he felt himself step on something solid.

"Ouch!" someone yipped.

He took another step, and no one was around him. Suddenly he saw a figure rising out of the snow. The figure was shaped like a girl but glistening white. The figure began to shift, and the whiteness went away. Standing there was the tangerine-haired girl who had performed for him and the others over a month and a half ago.

"What just happened?" Connor asked.

"Oh, I was lying in the snow. I didn't see you approaching. I was admiring the tree," she explained as she pointed to the large red star.

"Were you under the snow? How did I miss you?" he inquired.

"Oh, ha-ha, I can change colors to match my surroundings."

Connor thought back to the first time he talked with Dr. Finn in the hove rover, "Like a lizard," he and the girl said at the same time.

"Precisely." She went on, "I'm very sorry, sometimes it happens, and I don't realize it."

"Oh, no, don't worry about it. I'm the one who should apologize. I stepped on your.... Well... I'm not sure what I stepped on," he replied with a hint of embarrassment.

She giggled a bit and smiled, "It's quite alright. I'm kind of cold now though; I'm going to the commons to warm up."

"Ok, bye then." He waved and slowly turned back towards the tree. He began to step lightly because he realized that in this place, anything could happen.

He got close to the tree and felt the rough branches. It wasn't real wood, but the sight was very convincing. He looked up at the tree and gazed at the red star sparkling. He saw an arm and head waving over the tree and the railing of the Registration room. He couldn't quite make it out, but he was convinced it was Mr. Templeton waving down at him. He waved back and started to admire the tree once again.

He thought and pondered. He theorized and wondered.... Nothing would come to him. He didn't feel any energy. He didn't have a clue. The only idea he had was to close his eyes and make a wish. This seemed like a good time to do it. "I wish I could find my Impetus. I wish I could find that part of myself so I can fit in with the others." Connor slowly opened his eyes half expecting to be whisked away to another place or to have his new ability.

He turned around and saw Natalie and Liam entering the snowball fight. He enjoyed the view of his joyful peers. He shrugged his shoulders, bent down, fashioned a ball of snow, and sprinted towards his cheerful allies.

The next evening, Liam, Connor, and Natalie were eating dinner in the café. They conversed while they enjoyed bowls of mulberry stew.

"The venison in this is my favorite," Liam said as he slurped liquid from the edge of his bowl.

"It is delicious. It tastes like the holidays," Natalie added.

Connor took a big scoop with his spoon and enjoyed the stew as it rolled over his tongue. The three noticed Mr. Templeton sitting two tables down when he began to laugh loudly as usual. He caught their eye and hopped up with pep in his step. He carried a large bucket in his arm. They weren't sure, but it looked like gallons of ginger nog.

"How does he do it?" Liam asked. "How can anyone enjoy that much of a warm beverage?"

"I don't know. Sometimes I feel like I could if I truly tried," Natalie chuckled.

"Happy Holiday! I'm so happy to say.... Happy, happy, happy, holiday!" Mr. Templeton sang a silly tune. "Ha ha ha! Did you hear?" he asked.

"Hear what?" Connor inquired.

"Word has it.... Your little friend Mr. Donaghue found his Impetus today," he whispered through his hand.

"What?!" Connor asked loudly. He had never felt happy and angry at the same time. He was agitated that he was now the only remaining brown robe.

"That's great news!" Liam said as Natalie agreed.

"Whelp… I'll see you all next time. I have to run." Mr. Templeton ran along down the rows of tables. He greeted others as he passed on his merry way.

"I gotta go," Connor muttered.

"Hey, wait," Liam said as he stood up with him.

"No," Connor replied as he stormed off.

Natalie looked at Liam as he sat back down with a slight frown. "Let him go."

Connor ran to the elevators and Liam and Natalie continued to eat as their table shifted from a deep emerald shade to a bright garnet shimmer. Connor raced through the Rotunda and into the Analysis Hall. He scampered down to Room 24 and started to knock on the door. He couldn't believe it. There had to be a mistake. The door opened, and there stood young Philip Donaghue with a proud smile and fresh yellow robes.

"I found it!" Philip spoke exuberantly.

"I see... I see.... What is it?" Connor asked.

"Ok. Ok. I'll tell you but keep it a secret," he said as he dragged Connor into the room. "Hardly anyone knows but here it goes," he said as he stepped back and paused for a moment. He closed his eyes and concentrated. Philip opened his mouth wide.

HONK!

Out of his mouth came a sound that resembled the horn from cars and hove rovers.

"Wow! You can honk like a car?" Connor asked a bit perplexed.

"That's not all, silly," he said in Natalie's exact voice.

"Whoa!" Connor asked, "You can make sounds? Mimic them?!"

Philip hung his head back, and a roaring thunder came out of his mouth and echoed through the room.

"Wow... I don't know what to say, Philip. Congratulations," he tried to keep a good attitude as he spoke.

"Thanks, Connor. Really... listen... I'm sure you'll get yours soon. It'll happen! I believe!" Philip encouraged him.

"I know... I know...." Connor continued, "I hope you're right. Oh, and don't worry. I won't say anything."

Connor smiled and nodded as he walked out and entered Room 22. He sat down on the lone chair and held his face in his hands. A few tears fell from his eye. He had never felt so alone. Suddenly, Eden felt like a torture facility rather than a place of solitude and protection. He leaned back in his chair and wiggled as if he was annoyed.

Connor took a long deep breath and looked up. He thought about his parents. The thought of them brought him relief. He imagined being home for the holidays and going to the park with his parents. The Recreation Room was far superior to the park near his house, but he still longed to be with them.

He walked over to his chest and entered his code into the display. He looked in to see a layer of brown robes. He dug around a bit and found the night light, the manual, and the model aircraft. He lifted the aircraft and smiled at the thought of Dr. Finn. He placed it back in the box and took out the night light and the manual. He sat down on the floor and closed the box tight.

Connor placed the night light on the box and turned it on. The glow was pleasing and reminded him of his mother's love. He caught the smell of the old book, and he grew calm. He opened the manual to the front page. It read:

Property of Andrew Laurel

He thumbed through the pages and browsed over diagrams explaining maneuvers to counter enemies in the air. There were diagrams of formations that were used to keep the squad safe. He saw tiny notations throughout the book where his great grandfather had written around the text.

He kept turning, and a note suddenly fell from the crease of another page. The note was old, and the words were pale blue. Connor imagined his father reading the letter to him.

To my Son,

Always be brave. Take up for others who are less fortunate than you. Trust your instincts when it matters most. Life is full of choices... don't let the bad ones define who you are. Prepare for the few moments when you'll be tested. Those are the times you'll be fulfilled and will find purpose. This manual helped me to be the best man I could be... I pass it on to you because I know you're ready to be a man.

Above all, remember that living is about giving, not receiving.

I love you.

-Dad

Connor had never felt so ashamed. He knew that his jealousy and impatience were bad for him. He was inspired by the note and realized that his father passed this same message to him. He hadn't received his Impetus yet, and for the first time, he truly didn't care. He wanted to be a man who found ways to give to others rather than waiting to receive. He took the book and night light and placed them in the box, and with a peaceful heart, he went to sleep.

Holiday

The next day, Connor still felt peaceful and hopeful. His ornament vibrated, and he received a message from Natalie. "Don't forget, today we're all going to the assembly hall for a movie," her voice played.

He missed the last movie due to riding Liam's hove bike carelessly in the Recreation room. He did not want to miss another so he decided to be extra good that day. He met the others for lunch in the café and enjoyed wrapped lamb with glazed pecans.

"Has anyone seen Philip? I thought we would have seen him by now," Natalie said.

Connor responded trying to keep his promise, "I haven't."

"Maybe he can become invisible?! He could be here right now," Liam suggested. He stretched his arm around him and along the bench trying to feel the possible phantom. "Guess not, ya know… I'm ready to go home tomorrow."

"I'll be here all alone for a week," Natalie responded.

"No, you won't," Connor said, "I'll be here next week as well."

"Really?! But why?" Natalie asked.

"I have to get scanned more. I'll only get a week at home. It'll be nice to have each other around I suppose."

"Why yes, I was afraid I would be stuck alone the whole week," Natalie replied.

They finished their meal and made their way to the Assembly Hall.

"I really hope Philip doesn't miss the movie," Natalie said as they sat in their seats in the first balcony.

The railing in front of them, the walls, and the ceiling were decorated with artificial holly, and the aroma of coffee and caramel flowed around them. Everyone in Eden was seemingly present, and there wasn't an empty seat to be found. Even the professors were scattered around the room. The lights went dim, and a single area on the front of the stage was lit as if by candlelight. Professor Ozil made his way from the side of the stage and stood in front of the curtain wearing a green and stylish red suit.

"Welcome everyone." He brushed his hair back with his hand. "You all will be leaving tomorrow for the holiday. The staff and I wanted to commend you on the great behavior and hard work that you have done thus far. I'm happy to say that it's been ten semesters since our last disturbance."

Connor looked at the other two inquisitively. They each looked back and shrugged.

"You'll all be home for a couple of weeks, and we ask that you enjoy it! It is imperative that we all get a little rest from time to time. We wish you the happiest of holidays!" The Professor took a step back towards the side of the stage and stopped. "Oh... I nearly forgot! Before we start the film, we will have a very special performance from one of our students," he concluded and walked off the stage.

The dark, green stiff curtain rose slowly. Standing behind it was none other than the young Philip Donaghue.

"Is that Philip?!" Liam asked.

Natalie added, "What is he doing?"

He stood there for a moment in the dim lone light and finally spoke aloud. "This... Is... A special song.... For a... a... Very special lady...." Philip looked towards the right, middle section. He began staring and smiling at the girl with the ocean blue robes and tangerine hair. Her friends giggled around her, and in her embarrassment, her arms and legs began to match her seat. Philip opened his mouth, and the warmest, smoothest male voice began to sing a holiday song. The crowd was astonished that this voice was coming from this young boy wearing yellow robes.

"Is this a trick?" Liam asked.

"No, he can mimic. That's his Impetus," Connor whispered to both of them.

They leaned back in awe along with the rest of the auditorium. The tangerine-haired girl began to smile, and she returned to her natural form. Philip finished the song and took a bow. With a crack in his normal voice, he said cheerfully, "Thank... thank you." He then awkwardly ran off the stage. The assembly applauded him, and some of them laughed over his comical exit.

Connor didn't feel remorse and was happy for Philip even though he was now the only brown robe in the entire Assembly Hall. The holiday movie played on and when it finished, the young operators spent the rest of the day in the winter wonderland down in the Recreation room.

All of the operators left Eden the next day. Only Dr. Finn, Natalie, and Connor remained along with a handful of professors and staff. Natalie and Connor spent most of the mornings playing chess and reading in the common rooms. They shared every meal with Mr. Templeton who made the empty café echo with each word he spoke. Sometimes they enjoyed his company and other times they did not. Dr. Finn remained in his office but would walk and talk with them in the Rotunda when he could.

Connor spent each afternoon and night in Room 22 being scanned. He sat on the floor, he sat on the reclining chair, he stood, he sat on his box, and he played with the digital dragon on his ornament and repeated the process. Enduring the pale light shining for hours at a time was nearly maddening.

He read his flight manual. He practiced the techniques he learned from combative training and even recited different commands from tactics class. Natalie would visit from time to time but never stayed long. The room was built to scan one person. Her father explained this to her earlier in the year.

It was the last evening and night that Connor had to sit before leaving for home the next morning. He was happy to be going home but dreaded one more night of sitting and sleeping in that lonely room. He went through his same old process to pass the time and eventfully fell asleep on the reclining chair.

Clog. Clog. Clog. Clack. Clog. Clog. Clog. Clack.

Connor opened his eyes and yawned a bit. He rubbed his face and looked down at his ornament. It read 2:19 am in a dull glow. He was awoken by the clogging and clacking outside of the door. He slowly stood up and walked towards the exit. He placed his hand on the door, and the door opened. He heard the noise echoing far down the hall and saw lights from the Rotunda shining through the dark corridor.

Exiting the corridor and into the rotunda was a white figure. He rubbed his eyes again and looked both ways down the hallway. "What?" he asked himself. The figure left his vision as it entered the Rotunda.

In a brief whim of bravery, he decided to sneak towards the Rotunda. "I'm tired of that dumb room anyways," he whispered to himself. He moved quickly and quietly to the Rotunda and noticed the figure walking slowly and steadily towards the escalators. He followed along at a quicker pace. He went up the first escalator and noticed the figure round a corner from his sight.

Connor walked and got near the edge of the corner. He put his back to the wall. He slid down to the floor and slowly peeked around the corner. The area was dark, but he noticed a person wearing white robes and black boots seemingly with its hand in the wall. The figure made a small racket and pulled its arms from out of the wall. A panel came down and closed. The figure started to walk back towards Connor, and he grew nervous. He stopped peeking around the corner.

Clog. Clog. Clog. Clack. Clack. Clack.

The noise of the person walking sounded closer and closer. Connor was frightened. The sound stopped. It began again, but the sound started to lose volume. Connor peeked around the corner again and saw the figure a bit clearer as it walked away. It was a man. He wore tight white robes and the dark boots.

Connor felt his arm vibrate and a panic came over him. He held it closer, and the familiar voice spoke, "Please return to Room 22." He was frightened that his ornament may have given his position away. He stood up quickly and sprinted back to the room without looking back. Out of breath he sat down near his box and tried to relax. Connor sat for a few minutes and then returned to the reclining chair. He pondered who the person could have been, and he didn't sleep any more that night.

Hours passed, and Connor heard a knock at the door. He expected the white robed figure would be standing there waiting for him. The door opened and there stood Colonel Albert wearing the same clothes and trench coat he had worn on the first day they met. "Come," the Colonel commanded.

They walked down to the nearest elevator and Natalie was standing there waiting. They greeted one another, and the three stood in the elevator. "Receptacle," Colonel Albert spoke.

They arrived in the same hallway that Connor had entered months earlier. They walked down the long hallways and entered the landing bay. Connor looked up towards the window expecting General Marks to be watching them leave but the room above was empty. The Colonel spoke into his ornament, and a hove rover rolled on the tracks from a dark tunnel. Machine arms reached down and placed it facing the opening.

They all got in the car. The colonel drove them down the area for a while, and the car gently lifted from the surface and flew out of Eden. Natalie and Connor looked out of their windows to see Eden and the Edifice rotating above. The clouds seemed to devour the structure as they climbed into the sky.

"He's going to drop you first. Then he's going to take me to my aunt's," Natalie explained.

"Good. No problem." Connor was about to tell Natalie about the person he encountered last night but froze. He looked up to the front of the car and remembered the Colonel's Impetus.

"Exceptional hearing," he murmured.

"What was that?" she asked.

"Interesting earrings," he replied.

She felt her ears and touched her tiny earrings. "Oh... thanks," she said seeming a bit confused.

"So, where's your father?" Connor asked.

"Oh, he was going to come with me to my aunt's house. But he said he had to stay to work on next semester's class material."

"Yeh, you're probably right," Connor assured her. He had a sinking feeling that it may have to do with the person roaming around

Eden last night. The car flew on for a few hours, and then they descended. They drove onto Connor's old street, and he was full of anticipation. He got out of the car and waved goodbye to Natalie and walked up to his doorstep. The house was decorated with holiday lights, and mistletoe hung over the front door.

Connor quietly opened the door and heard his parents talking in the kitchen. He caught the smell of cinnamon and marshmallows.

"I'm home!" he shouted.

The speech went silent in the kitchen, and his parents came running towards him. They nearly tackled him as they gave him hugs and a kiss on the head. They directed him to the kitchen where they all ate freshly baked cookies. Connor was happy to be home after a very long time away.

Three days passed and Connor continued to wonder about the strange person at Eden. He was standing in his bedroom and caught a glimpse outside through his window. The ground was lightly powdered with snow from the night before. He noticed Samantha bouncing around inside of her home round a Christmas tree. She had shorter hair but seemed to have the same amount of endless energy.

"Come downstairs, sweetie!" his mother's voice resounded from the family room. He went downstairs and saw his parents sitting around their modest tree. It was real and shorter than Connor. It was trimmed with colorful threads and glass bulbs. It was Christmas morning.

"Now I wanted to send this to you earlier but it took me longer to finish than I expected," Sybil said handing him a crimson wrapped package. "So it's a Christmas gift now!"

He quickly opened it and held it in front of him. It was a navy jacket with ribbed sleeves and a round collar. He actually thought it was trendy and tried it on. It felt perfect in the chest and back, but the sleeves were a little short.

"See... I told you he'd be taller than we remembered," Timothy said with a smile.

"Here... let me see..." Sybil said as she helped him adjust the jacket. "Take off your wrist watch. It's making it tight around your arm," she instructed.

"Oh, I'm sorry, mom. I can't.... It's not a watch, it's a monitor..." he replied.

She gave him a sad look and kissed him on the head. "You poor boy. The jacket looks fine as it is."

"Thanks mom, I love it."

"Ok, now take a look at this," his father said as he handed him a flat white box.

Connor opened it carefully and inside he found four tickets to the Briar's museum. "They had such a big turnout from the exhibit simulation thingy. They decided to keep it around. We're going tomorrow!" he said excitedly.

"Wow, that's fantastic! Who is the 4th ticket for?" he asked holding the tickets in hand.

Sybil explained, "Well, Samantha keeps asking about you, and we thought it'd be nice to invite her along. I hope that's ok."

"No, that's good. That's quite alright."

"Splendid," his mother concluded.

Christmas Day continued with all of its pleasantries and early the next day they went to the museum.

The family and Samantha arrived at a large building with marble steps and tall steel columns. They walked inside to see a display showing an image of a young woman dressed like a pilot. She instructed them to insert their tickets into the box underneath the display. They dropped their tickets in one by one and a door opened for the four of them to pass through.

Connor walked with his family through rooms of statues, paintings, and exhibits. Samantha skipped around in circles occasionally as they walked. They came upon a group of museum visitors huddled around a central section of the atrium. Connor passed through the crowd and saw an area roped off by burgundy ropes. It separated the visitors from the device in the center. In the middle sat a capsule that reminded Connor of the one from Aviation class. This device was much more primitive and a bit smaller. The crowd watched displays that sat upon narrow stands. They could see what the person inside the capsule was seeing and could see the person's face.

A man with a large mustache and short, buzzed hair was operating the simulation. Another older man was within the capsule seemingly sitting in an aircraft flying itself. The simulation ended, and the old man crawled out of the device.

"Very good! You could have taken control. You didn't have to use autopilot the entire time," the mustached man explained. "Any other volunteers?!"

Connor and a few others raised their hands. Luckily, the man chose Connor and signaled him over to the capsule.

"Good luck!" Samantha shouted.

Connor looked back to see his parents grinning at him. He stepped into the capsule and the man closed him inside. "You'll have five minutes, and I'll start you in the air. Let's see.... Ah, we'll do this one."

The screens inside showed him flying over a desert with large mounds of sand rolling as far as the eye could see. The craft alerted him that he was in autopilot mode. He sat and thought for a moment. Connor took over the controls and switched off the autopilot.

"Looks like he found the off switch!" the mustached man said loudly to the crowd. He chuckled because he assumed Connor's move was beginner's luck. Connor cracked a smile and increased the throttle. He started to dive towards the ground and increased speed swiftly. Right before he crashed into the ground he pulled the control stick back and steadied the craft. He could hear the crowd gasp from the outside. He then turned the craft upside down and flew that way for a moment.

He confidently tilted it back over to its natural side and began to climb. For the next four minutes, he practiced maneuvers that he read about in his grandfather's manual. The simulation ended, and the capsule grew dark. The top popped open, and he began trotting proudly towards his parents. The mustached man announced, "I've never seen anything like that!"

Connor continued over to Timothy, Sybil, and Samantha.

"He's a natural! Just like his granddad!" Timothy shouted to Sybil.

"Wow... Connor.... That was Sooo great!!!" Samantha said in adoration.

"Thanks," Connor replied with confidence.

The crowd couldn't keep their eyes off Connor. They were baffled. The family and Samantha continued to make their way through the large museum. After making another round, they decided to leave and returned home.

Two more days passed and it was time for Connor to return to Eden. He stood outside of his front door wearing his new navy jacket as he watched the hove rover arrive on his street. Connor got into the car and was taken back to his home away from home. The whole way flying back to Eden he thought of the great time he had with his parents. When he caught sight of the large pyramid glistening in the distance, a crushing reality began to poison his joyful thoughts. A strange man was prowling around Eden.

<u>Secret</u>

When Connor arrived in Eden, he hoped he would be able to join Liam in the bunks once again. Unfortunately, his ornament directed him back to Room 22. Connor returned to the scanning room and placed the new jacket in his chest. He changed out of his clothes and into the brown robes.

"Hey! Did you miss me?!" Liam joked as he stood in the door way of Room 22.

Connor ran over and gave him a friendly hug and taunted him, "I missed General Marks more." They chuckled and talked about their holiday away from Eden. They made their way through the Rotunda and to the elevators.

"Liam, I want to tell you something. Something I saw," Connor said.

"Ok, shoot."

"I can't here, it would have to be in private," Connor explained.

"I hope you're not thinking of getting me in trouble, pal. I suffered from a stressful situation last semester. I'm not sure I can take another one," he joked. "I'm only kidding... can it wait though? I'm starving!"

"Sure," Connor agreed as they entered the café.

The boys gobbled up dinner and decided to go to the commons room. Once they were there, they discovered Natalie talking with a few other yellow and blue robed girls.

"Nat!" Liam shouted.

"It's so good to see you two again," she responded with a big smile, "How was the trip, Connor?"

"It was good. It felt shorter on the way back," he replied.

"We get a month of Impetus training before we start classes again, have you been assigned anywhere?" Natalie asked.

"Um, no... not yet."

"Oh, well I'm sure something will come up," Natalie finished.

They sat down and played a few games on their tablets and then returned to their quarters for the night. After long hours of scanning, Connor thought of an idea.

"Record," he spoke into his ornament. "Colonel Albert, I was wondering if we could train. I haven't found my Impetus yet, and classes don't start for a month. It's ok if you don't have any free time, but I thought I'd ask."

"Send to Daniel Albert."

Moments later, Connor's ornament vibrated.

"Message received," the ornament spoke.

"Play."

"7:00 am. Meet me in the training room," Colonel Albert's voice played, and the message ended.

The next day, Connor went into the training room. He stood on the mat and stretched his legs. Colonel Albert came in behind him. "I'll only have a few hours in the mornings," he explained. He spoke into his ornament, and a tray came out of the ceiling. It held two long training sticks. The Colonel took them off the tray, and the tray ascended into the ceiling. He passed one to Connor who bobbled at it first before gripping it tightly.

"Today, I feel like working with weapons. Is that satisfactory?" Colonel Albert asked.

"Yes, sir," Connor replied.

They started practicing different stances and strikes with the sticks as they held them with both hands. They trained for a couple of hours and ended with a bow to one another. Connor met Liam, Natalie, and Philip in the café for a meal. Shortly after, Connor was directed back to Room 22. He practiced what he learned in the lonely room until it was time to go to bed.

Connor trained with the Colonel every morning until the end of the week. On the last day, Connor and the Colonel stretched their bodies and sat quietly for a moment to cool down from the workout. As the Colonel stood up and prepared to leave, Connor asked him a question.

"Colonel, on the night before you took me home, before the holiday," Connor felt that he could trust the Colonel because of the time he was investing in him. He went on, "I woke up at 2:00 am or very close to it. And outside of my door passed a man in a white robe."

The Colonel paused and turned to look at Connor. He listened as Connor continued.

"I followed the person through the Rotunda, and then up the escalator-"

"You're not supposed to be out after curfew, Mr. Laurel," the Colonel interrupted him.

"Yes I know sir, but something felt wrong. I've never heard anyone outside of my door before."

The Colonel sighed. "Continue."

"I saw him turn a corner and I hid to see what was happening. He looked like he was working on something in the wall. And then he disappeared into the darkness. I've been by that wall before, and I've never noticed anything unusual there," Connor explained.

The Colonel questioned, "Who else knows about this?"

"No one sir, I haven't gotten a chance to tell anyone. I didn't even want you to know really. I was afraid I would be in trouble. But, I had to tell someone."

"No, no, you're not in trouble yet… stay in your room next time though. Don't tell anyone else about this. Keep it to yourself," the Colonel instructed.

"What about Dr. Finn?" Connor asked.

"I'll talk to him. I need you to keep this quiet though. We don't need this getting out to everyone," the Colonel told him.

"Yes, sir. Whatever you think is best."

"I'll see you next week if you haven't found your Impetus in the next two off days. Perhaps you'll find it before classes begin." The Colonel talked as he moved towards the door, "Connor... did this person have an ornament?" he asked standing in the doorway.

"Now that you mention it, sir... I didn't see one."

"Interesting. Goodbye now," the Colonel said as he walked away.

Connor wasn't sure if he had made a mistake or did the right thing by telling the Colonel. The mystery made him nervous, but he was afraid to bring any extra attention to the subject.

Weeks passed by and Connor continued to train and read his old flight manual. He would see Liam, Natalie, Philip, and some of the others during meals. They would play or converse on off days. Most of the conversations were about Impetus training.

Classes had started again, and Connor grew more worried about spending an eternity in the scanning room rather than being with his friends. It felt cruel to him. Not only did he not have an Impetus but he was also ostracized. Connor was in the common rooms before evening classes were about to begin when he received a message on his ornament. It was Dr. Finn.

"Connor, come see me in my office before you head to combative training," the message played. Connor went to Dr. Finn's office to meet him.

"Welcome, Connor. Please take a seat. Something to drink?"

Connor replied, "No, thanks, sir. I'm not thirsty."

"Very well."

Dr. Finn walked past his dark green desk and leaned in to speak. "Connor, I'm proud of you for being so resilient this year. Staying in the scanning room for as long as you have is not the norm. I was checking the records, and there have only been a few operators who have taken this long to find their Impetus once they arrived at Eden."

"Why is that, sir? What's different?" Connor asked.

"No one quite knows, Connor. By the time someone has been scanned this much, the system usually has enough information to pinpoint the source of the operator's energy," he continued.

"So, what do we know about me? Are there any clues?" Connor inquired.

"So far, we don't have any clues."

Connor groaned with frustration, "There must be a mistake. I'm probably not even an operator."

"No, no, no that would be impossible. I promise you, Connor. In time, your Impetus will be made clear."

Connor was still at peace about being a brown robe, but he longed for the scanning to stop. He wanted to return to the bunks with the others.

"Connor," the doctor said as his voice lowered in volume and increased in sincerity. "The Colonel told me about the night you saw the strange person."

Connor leaned in, "Am I in trouble?"

"Heavens no... but I wanted you to know that he told me."

"Do you know who it was, sir… who the person was that night?" Connor asked softly.

"We can't be sure, but we have an idea. I want you to message me any time day or night if you hear or see them again. I mean it. Day or night. Let me know," Dr. Finn beckoned him.

"Absolutely, sir. Anything to help."

"Very good!" the doctor said in a louder and brighter tone. He stood up from his desk and loosened his posture. The two of them continued to talk about Connor's classes and training exercises. Connor eventfully caught up with the rest of his group and moved on to Aviation class.

"In the first semester, you learned how to fly your craft. You learned how to fly it safely. This semester we will begin using weaponry," Captain Brookmeyer elucidated, "You will practice against one another. I will break you into squads next week, but first I have a special assignment for each of you. I want you to design or choose your craft. The capsules will simulate your flight based on standard dimensions and speeds of course, but I believe that your ship is an extension of yourself while in the air. I have worked with Mr. Templeton on this. I want you to feel as much like a real pilot as possible. We will scan your design and implement it into your craft during the simulation." The captain continued, "You can find models in your text, design your own, or check the archives in the References Room."

"I'm not very good at drawing," Natalie whispered to Connor and Liam.

"I'm sure we'll figure something out," Liam whispered back.

Connor pondered as the lecture continued. He was looking forward to flying as much as he could. He felt more comfortable in the capsule than he did in the scanning room. After the class ended, Liam and Connor went down to References.

Liam spoke into his ornament, "Find aircrafts."

"Forty-five matches," his ornament announced.

"Wow... I may be here for the rest of the night."

"I'm sure you will find something that you like soon," Connor replied.

Liam turned and asked, "What about you, what are you going to do about your craft design?"

A notion entered Connor's head. "I think I know exactly what I'm going to do."

The week passed by as usual. Connor was being scanned at night, and he was trying to spend time with his peers as much as possible. He was practically obsessed with the idea of using the capsules more this semester. It was almost time to turn in the design for Aviation class. Connor walked through the Rotunda with the model of the K-13 Rex he had obtained his first day.

The children entered the room, and they all brought photographs and diagrams on their tablets for Mr. Templeton to scan.

"Come one, come all! Don't be shy!" Mr. Templeton shouted as he slapped the Captain on the back. The students cheerfully lined up one by one as Mr. Templeton used a small handheld scanner to upload their models to their ornaments.

"You will be able to view this whenever you want. Just say *My Craft* into your ornament, and it will appear," he said as he went on scanning each tablet. "Oh, I like that Dominic!" Dominic's aircraft was pitch black and shaped like a thin triangle. It had twin, blue engines resting vertically on the back.

Connor finally reached the front of the line and he held up his model. "That is something special..." The Captain said, "I never had a chance to fly one of those."

"Ha-ha-ha! Very old school, Mr. Laurel, but I like it!" Mr. Templeton shouted as he scanned the model. The remainder of the students scanned their vehicles, and Mr. Templeton made his way out of the room. Connor grew increasingly excited about Aviation class. While he was in the class, he never thought about Room 22 or the strange white robed man.

Goal

More days passed and the group became more comfortable with their aircrafts. They hadn't competed but simply practiced flying in formation and shooting simulated targets. After class, the group was heading for the common room to socialize until dinner. As they entered the Rotunda, they ran into Liam's cousin walking out of the Infirmary.

"This is bad... this is bad," the boy in the ocean blue robe was chanting outside of the Infirmary.

"Hey, Zane. What's wrong?!" Liam asked as Connor and Natalie followed behind.

"It's my football team. We're done for now."

"Wait, wait, slow down," Liam calmed him.

"Our best midfielder hurt his knee in practice today. We have a game tomorrow, and we don't have anyone to replace him," Zane discussed.

"Well, that's too bad, " Liam responded and started walking away.

"Wait! Wait... I know you're only thirteen but you're pretty strong. Come play with us! Please!!! I'm your cousin," Zane begged.

"Haha. Come on. You know soccer isn't my bag. I'm horrible with my feet."

"I love football!" Natalie piped up.

Zane completely ignored her comment and saw Connor. "What about you? You can play right?" Zane looked him up and down. "You seem to have a good center of gravity."

"Um... sure I guess; I used to kick a ball back home."

"Perfection!" Zane interrupted. "Come down to the recreation room tomorrow at 4 o'clock."

"One condition," Connor made the boy freeze. "You let Natalie play too."

"Alright, alright... I'll send you both a jersey. I don't expect she'll get any play time, but she can dress all the same," Zane explained.

"Deal," Connor said as he shook the boy's hand.

The next day, Connor arrived on the field wearing a shiny silver jersey with the number 22 on his chest. *Just my luck. The number of my tomb...* he thought to himself. The field was well lit by the beam of light falling through the Registration Room. The field had white lines and goals on either end. A group of operators stood on the opposite side of the field in shiny black jerseys.

Connor found Liam and Natalie on his own sideline.

"Hey! You look metallic," Liam said jokingly.

"Thanks... I guess?" Connor replied.

Natalie was standing by Liam wearing a jersey as well. She waited patiently for the game to begin.

"Oh! Awesome! You're here!" Zane said victoriously. "You'll be starting in the midfield. If you get the ball, don't be nervous. Just try to pass it to the striker."

Connor ran onto the field and felt a bit nervous. He had never played this game before, and there were plenty of operators watching from the sideline. The other team ran onto the field, and Connor uttered, "Oh no." He saw Dominic jogging onto the field and towards the other team's net. Connor kept jogging onto the field, and he felt a stinging pain on the side of his foot. "Sssssssss," he hissed as he started to hobble and reached down towards his foot.

"Faking injuries already, nugget?!" Dominic shouted from his net. Plenty of operators began to laugh as Zane came sprinting up to Connor.

"What's wrong? What happened?!" he asked frantically.

"I'm not sure. I just sprang it a bit," Connor replied.

"Can you play?!" Zane shouted.

Connor's pain quickly left, and he wiggled his foot around.

"Um, yeh. I think I'll be fine."

"Good. Walk around a bit; it's almost time," Zane rushed him.

A horn sounded throughout the coliseum, and the game began. The ball was well fought for in the middle of the field, but Connor could hardly keep up. He barely understood the rules of the game. Liam shouted from the sideline, "Come on! Let's go team!"

"Not your bag, eh?" Natalie said as she stretched and bounced around.

He replied, "I just want Connor to do well, that's all."

Connor struggled as he had given away the ball every time he dribbled it. He caught the sight of Dominic laughing as he tended his team's goal. The other team seemed quite professional as they passed and juked down the field. Their striker found an opening and knocked the ball in the back of Connor's net using his head. Their team celebrated, and the room projected a large *1-0* above them.

"That's ok; we have plenty of time left!" Zane shouted to the rest of his team.

The ball went back, forth, up and down the field. Connor's team pushed forward into the enemies' territory, and he found himself inside their box. The ball was deflected towards him when he formed a stiff demeanor. He had an open shot but felt peer pressure all over him.

"Shoot!" Zane cried as the ball rolled towards Connor.

Defenders were sprinting as quickly as possible towards him. Connor suddenly visualized kicking the ball at the brick wall back home. He took a breath and kicked the ball as hard as he possibly could. The ball curved through the air at a high rate as Dominic dove to deflect it. The ball hit Dominic's hand and flew into the top right corner of the net. At that moment a defender was attempting a sliding tackle and impacted directly into Connor's left leg.

Connor flipped and rolled on the ground, and the defender jumped up with regret. The room projected *1-1*. The room glowed yellow and projected the number *3* which was the jersey number of the player who fouled Connor. Connor's teammates ran over to celebrate and lifted him off the field. Zane and another operator locked shoulders with Connor and helped him over to the side lines.

Connor assured them, "I'm fine. I just need to sit for a moment." His ankle started to swell.

"We only have ten players now," Zane panicked.

Natalie cleared her throat, "Eh hmmphh!"

"Oh yeh, ok... you can go in. Just try to pass it around," Zane explained.

"Nice shot," Liam said as he sat down by Connor. "Think they'll have to remove it?" he teased as he pointed to Connor's left leg.

"Hahaha... Perhaps..."

Natalie and the rest of the team scurried onto the field. Time passed and only ten minutes remained in the game. Natalie hadn't touched the ball yet.

"Pass it to, Natalie!" Liam and Connor shouted. It was almost the end of the game, and they felt it wouldn't do any harm to allow her to make a clean pass. Natalie seemed fed up with the current state of the game and made a sprint towards the ball.

"Hey! Go back to your position!" Zane yelled across the field.

Natalie made a clever tackle and stole the ball. She started to dribble and to the entire field's surprise, she wasn't bad. She was actually phenomenal.

She twisted and turned. She sprinted and stopped. She dribbled the ball between a defender's legs, and he fell over in confusion. She ran along the side line kicking the ball making it seem like the defense was standing in place. She found a small opening near the goal and illusively shot the ball too far out of Dominic's reach. She had just scored an impressive goal. The operators on the sidelines celebrated and shouted. Her team ran to her jumping and shouting as she jumped up and down.

"I wasn't expecting that," Connor said.

"My friend, no one was expecting that," Liam agreed as he clapped his hands and whistled.

Dominic's face started to glow blood red, and his mouth frowned as if he had been cheated. "Well, I guess that makes sense then! All of that twisting and turning. No wonder you killed your mom when you were born!!" Dominic shouted for the whole field to hear.

Natalie fell to her knees as if she'd just been impaled. Her mouth dropped open, and her eyes started to water. The celebrations fell quiet, and Dominic glared at her.

"Aaaaaaaaaaaaaaagggggggggggggghhhhhhh hhh!!!!!!!!!!!!!!!" Dominic heard as he turned around to see Liam running towards him. Dominic just smirked as he watched Liam sprint his way. Liam, with all of his might, planted his left leg and swung his arm around to strike Dominic on the chin. Liam grabbed his hand and started screaming as he fell to the ground in agony. Dominic laughed at him as he watched him wallow on the field.

"Didn't you know my Impetus? My skin is stronger than metal, you twit." Dominic said menacingly.

Connor hobbled onto the field and helped Liam up.

"Look at you three. You're pathetic. I hope you all end up like Alexander," he said trying to insult them. Suddenly a large projection of General Malinda Marks covered the arena.

"Connor Laurel, Natalie Finn, Liam Hudson, and Dominic Knight come to the Registration Room Immediately," the message played. The operators on and along the field were astonished at what they had just heard and witnessed. It seemed as if Connor would have to endure an icy meeting with the infamous General Marks once again.

Punishment

Dominic, Connor, Liam, and Natalie sat on two separate sofas in the General Mark's office with their heads hanging down. General Marks scowled at them from her towering desk chair. "After our last meeting, I thought I wouldn't dare see you in the Master Room again. I suppose that every group, no matter how large or small has a bad apple or two," she scolded them as she stood up and walked towards the sofas.

"Mr. Knight and Ms. Finn, this is your first occurrence. I will warn you like I warned *these* two last semester. If you don't find a way to stay out of trouble, I will make you wish you had never come to Eden. It is my duty to make sure everyone in this facility stays civil. If you make that task difficult, I will make your every move difficult. Is that clear?!" she shouted.

"Yes, ma'am," they each stuttered.

Connor piped up, "General. Natalie didn't do anything! She was only playing the game."

"SILENCE! You know how speaking works in this office," she shouted again.

She walked over to Connor and Liam. General Marks quickly grabbed Liam's damaged hand tightly.

"Ouch!" he yipped in fright. As she held his hand his fingers begin to feel numb for a moment. She let go and he looked at his hand. He twisted it and turned it. It was as if he had never punched Dominic. "Sissy," she mumbled. She bent down and held Connor's leg. It hurt for a moment and then the swelling disappeared.

She continued, "Mr. Hudson, this is your second occurrence. You will be suspended from your classes for a week."

"But he has squad practice in aviation this week!" Connor interrupted.

"DO!!! NOT!!! INTERRUPT ME!!!" she shrieked.

"Since your companion keeps disrespecting my wishes Mr. Hudson, you will both be suspended for a week in which you will remain in your rooms. That's right Mr. Hudson, you will be staying in a room like Mr. Laurel. Alone and without your chests."

They each looked at each other in horror over their punishment.

"Now get out of my sight!" she exclaimed.

The four operators stood up and walked towards the doorway.

She spoke once again but with a lower tone, "Not you... Mr. Knight. Sit back down." Dominic returned to the sofa, and the door closed behind Connor and the others.

"She's impossible... I don't feel sorry for Dominic. He's a monster and deserves everything he gets," Liam said.

"Stop it," Natalie replied.

Connor spoke up, "She *is* wicked."

"She healed you two, didn't she?" Natalie had made a point.

"I suppose so, but solitary confinement isn't so sweet," Liam mentioned.

"That's my life, I'm afraid," Connor responded, "Natalie, where did you learn to play football like that?"

"Oh, it's nothing. I've been playing since I was nine. I've missed it really," she said.

"Well, it was fantastic," Liam claimed.

They entered the elevator, and Connor said, "Reserves… I can't believe it. He's like Draken," Connor said with remorse.

"His skin was extremely hardened," Liam went on, "Isn't that just great? That pathetic loser has a power of your favorite hero, and you don't even have your Impetus yet. How is this life fair?!"

Natalie scorned him, "Liam. Quiet down. You're being silly." The doors opened, and they walked into the hall.

"I'm going to eat," Liam said as he walked off vigorously.

"And I'll be taking a shower," Natalie said as she started towards her bunk.

Connor stopped her, "Hey... wait.... You're ok, right? You know, about what Dominic said."

"Yes, it was very rude and hurtful, but I'll be fine," she replied with a resilient smile.

"Good! By the way, who is Alexander? That dimwit said that bit at the end," he asked her.

"I'm not quite sure. But I'll ask my father. He'll probably know."

Connor gave her a nod, "Ok, good. I'll see you at dinner. I'm going to change."

They parted ways and didn't see each other again until they sat down for dinner.

After they had eaten and tried to forget about meeting with General Marks, Liam and Connor were directed to Room 22 and Room 24. They each sat in their rooms disgusted by their new arrangements. Connor was missing a week of class, and all of his work would have to be made up. This doubled his work for the following week.

He wanted to read his manual or play with his model aircraft, but his chest would not respond. It seemed to be without power. Connor got up from his reclined chair to stretch his legs. He decided to walk down the hall a bit to Liam's room. He and Liam timed their meetings, and they discovered they could be gone for anywhere from eight to ten minutes before their ornaments would agitate them. It would vibrate and direct them to their assigned location.

Connor and Liam had just started to speak when Natalie came marching down the hall. "Come you two. My father wants to talk to us." They followed her down the hall and into Dr. Finn's office.

"Hello," Dr. Finn greeted them.

They each greeted him back, and Connor and Natalie took a seat while Liam leaned on the back of Connor's chair.

"I wanted to speak to you all about the other day. You have to learn to control yourselves. You can't react rashly every time somcone offends you," he looked at Liam. "Natalie tells me that Dominic spouted off a name to each of you last week."

"Yes, sir. Alexander," Liam spoke up.

"Ah yes," the Doctor replied.

"Who is he?" Connor asked.

"He was talking about Alexander Page. He was a talented Operator. He wore red robes if I remember correctly."

Natalie inquired, "What happened?"

"Five years ago, Alexander did something very dangerous. He removed his ornament while he was at his home and told his parents all about Eden. These ornaments are not easy to remove. It's puzzling to think of how he did it." He went on as he pointed to his own ornament. "As you know, that is probably the worst thing you can do as an operator. He was highly sought after when that happened."

Liam asked, "How did he avoid being brought back? How did he not get caught?"

"He had quite a curious Impetus. He could pass through walls as if they weren't there. On top of that, he seems to be quite good at avoiding detection altogether."

"So what happened? How did Dominic hear about this?" Connor added.

"Well, Connor, we suspect you may have seen Alexander," Dr. Finn revealed.

"What?!" they all three exclaimed in unison.

Dr. Finn went on to explain what Connor had experienced on that night right before his holiday. "We think, that Alexander is somewhere in Eden. We don't know why yet… it is important that each of you report to me immediately if you see or hear anything unusual. We haven't had any operator harmed in Eden in a very long time so please don't be frightened," the doctor tried to assure them.

"Does everyone know about this, sir?" Connor asked.

"No, and we don't want a panic on our hands, so please keep quiet about it. General Marks had a long chat with Dominic similar to the one I'm having with you now. I doubt he'd be brave enough to cross her," he told them.

Natalie commented, "I don't get it, though; how did Dominic know about all of this in the first place?"

"We expect that Mr. Templeton probably gave it away on accident. He said he let slip the name *Alexander* at dinner a few weeks ago. Some of the older operators here remember Alexander, so a bit of questioning probably resulted in Dominic hearing a dramatic story. It's hard to keep secrets around here I've learned," Dr. Finn stated. "however, we're going to keep a close eye on Dominic just to be sure."

"I see," Connor exhaled.

"Ok, I have to prepare for Biology class tomorrow. You all run along now, and please… I beg you, stay out of trouble. You're missing a lot of material this week," he mentioned as he looked back and forth to Connor and Liam.

The three exited the room and continued to discuss what they had just discovered. They vowed to message each other if they saw anything unusual. Even if their reputations were seemingly becoming eradicated, they wanted to stay close and support one another.

Page

Time passed, and so did the suspension of Connor and Liam. They spent extra hours studying to catch up over the next few weeks.

"This formula just doesn't make sense? Why can't every class be like combative training? It seems much simpler to punch and block," Liam said. Connor, Philip, Liam, and Natalie sat in the café over a plum colored table. Liam was working on his tablet as the other three ate rosemary wrapped lamb with gooseberry pie.

"Speak for yourself! I think physics is much easier than combative class!" Philip countered.

Natalie and Connor each had their mouths full of pie listening to them talk.

Liam asked him with a serious tone, "How do you do it? How do you understand it so easily?"

"Because I have impeccable control over my mind, Mr. Hudson," Colonel Albert's voice came out of Philip's mouth. Connor choked a bit on the pie and Natalie snorted. Liam chuckled along as well. The young operators finished their meals and then went on to their evening classes.

"This week, you will face one another, it will be in the most challenging setting yet. We have covered every detail that you need to complete the mission. If you find that you're ill-equipped, then I suggest you spend extra time preparing for the battle. This will test your wits and your discipline. I will only tell you your basic task today, and you will need to meet with your squad mates to discuss formations and protocols," Captain Brookmeyer elucidated.

He continued to lecture the class, and most of the operators seemed intimidated by the upcoming activity. Connor, on the other hand, grew ecstatic. "Connor Laurel, Natalie Finn, and Liam Hudson, you will be squad G." Connor felt lucky to be paired with his friends. He thought it would give them a distinct advantage. The Captain continued grouping the operators.

"Squads A, C, E, and G will be offense. Squads B, D, F, and H will be defending. The rest of you will be paired and tested the following week. Offensive teams will have one craft with more devastating weaponry.

Defensive teams will have one craft with a cloaking device," he announced.

"Cloaking device, sir?" Philip asked.

"Yes, it will keep you invisible to your enemies until you show yourself or fire on them. It is based on the same technology that keeps Eden's location hidden," the captain informed them.

Connor spoke with Liam and Natalie, and they planned to spend the next day working on a plan to defeat the defending group. Connor released a deep sigh and went back up to Room 22. He felt cheated as he sometimes did. He still didn't have his Impetus, and it was early spring. He tried to keep it out of his mind. He felt more comfortable sleeping in the scanning room. It had become normal for him. He felt safer under the glow night after night.

He prepared for bed and decided to examine his aircraft. "My craft," he spoke. A three dimensional model of a K-13 Rex appeared and rotated over his ornament. He used his finger to rotate it so he could view the top and bottom with ease. He placed his fingers on its surface and zoomed into the craft to find details in the chassis. He put his ornament down by his side and closed his eyes.

A few minutes passed and his thoughts began to drift.

Beep… Beep… Beep… Beep… Beep… Beep…

He was nearly asleep when he heard a soft beep in the room. Connor looked back in the corner towards his chest, but it was quiet and dim. He looked towards the floor, and he saw a tablet pulsating soft light and dull beep.

He crawled off the reclined chair and looked around the room in fear. He didn't see anyone and was baffled by the tablet's sudden presence. He crept over to the tablet and sat down on the floor. He pressed the tablet's display, and the beeping subsided. A message read:

Hello, Connor. I am Alexander Page. Please be calm, and I won't hurt you. Write on the pad with your finger and wait.

Connor shivered at the thought that he may be in danger. He nervously placed his finger on the tablet and typed *O-K*.

An arm came through the wall and pulled the tablet to the other side. Connor was certain he was in a nightmare. A moment passed, and a hand delivered the tablet back through the wall.

Eden is not what it seems, Connor. It can be very dangerous. It has ruined me. Do you understand?

Connor felt frightened. He wrote back, *I don't understand. What are you talking about?* He wished that Liam or Natalie would show up in his room at any minute telling him it was a prank. An arm reached through the wall again and brought the tablet back to the other side.

The tablet came back through the wall.

Eden killed my parents.

Connor began to sweat. He suddenly thought about his own parents. He took a deep breath and thought maybe it was a lie. The only thing he could force himself to type was, *Why?*

The hand took the tablet. It placed it back on the floor.

That's what I'm here to find out.

Connor's mind had never been so muddled. He typed, *Why are you telling me this?*

The hand grabbed the tablet. The arm pushed it back through.

Because you're different… because the Edifice can't see you. Press play.

There was a tiny button at the bottom right of the display. Connor didn't want to do it. But he had no choice.

A video began to play. Dr. Finn was in his office sitting in one of his guest chairs. He had a drink in his hand sipping it slowly. General Marks was standing by the window looking towards Dr. Finn. The door was closed.

"How did he get in? Do we know?" Dr. Finn asked.

"I think he hid in a hove rover when one of the operators came back from the holidays. I cannot imagine how I would have missed it," she explained.

"Well, if he could go through walls years ago, we can assume he is more powerful now. I'm sure he could walk right through a hove rover. He doesn't have an ornament anymore. Still, it's hard to imagine how the Edifice wouldn't detect at least a trace of him," Dr. Finn continued.

She explained, "Ever since Connor has arrived, the system has been inconsistent, but it only seems to be inconsistent with him."

"It still can't see him? See his energy?" Dr. Finn asked.

"No, it can't. However, it wants to keep scanning. This has never happened in any of our records, and you know those go way back."

KNOCK! KNOCK! KNOCK!

"Come in!" Dr. Finn exclaimed.

Colonel Albert entered the room and saluted General Marks. "At ease," she commanded.

The Colonel reported, "I just spoke to Connor, he said he saw someone in white robes rummaging around the Rotunda during the holiday break."

"Could it be Page?" Dr. Finn asked.

"Perhaps. We have to keep scanning Connor. I don't want Alexander finding out about any of this if he is here."

"He won't like it, Malinda. He's just a boy. We're putting him in a prison. Isn't that the opposite of what we're trying to provide?" Dr. Finn spoke up.

"He may not like it, but it is necessary. I want both of you to give him extra attention. He trusts you," she said as she looked at Dr. Finn. "He trusts… both of you." She glanced at Colonel Albert. The Colonel saluted the General again and left the office.

"Ferdinand, you've been chosen for clearance," General Marks said.

"No… I... I don't know how it would help," he commented.

She took out large electronic keycard and placed it into his hand.

"It is necessary. These are the only two keycards. There's only ever been two. You know that. The Edifice thinks you're ready… you must protect this card with your life. It will allow you to go to the Edifice structure if you have any clues or want to sort your thoughts," she explained.

The transmission ended. Connor was overwhelmed. He felt like he had one thousand questions but not a single answer. He remembered being in the Master Room and watching General Marks using a keycard to shut the door behind her. He was in a panic trying to decide if the video was real. The hand grabbed the tablet and pulled it back through the wall.

It came back.

Will you help me?

Connor was confused. He didn't know who to trust, and he had no sense of security.

Connor typed into the tablet, *What do you need?*

The hand grabbed the tablet and pulled it through the wall.

It came back.

Meet me in the Recondite Room in two days at 4:00 pm.

Connor had never heard of the Recondite Room. He struggled with everything he had learned in such a short amount of time. He quickly typed, *Ok. I will.* The tablet was taken away. Connor waited for the tablet to return. He sat for ten or twenty minutes staring at the wall and was drenched in anxiety. He was confident that he would not sleep very well for the rest of the night.

Alpha

"Connor! Connor! Connor!"

Connor was in a trance as he looked over at Natalie and muttered, "Huh?"

"What's wrong with you today? We need to focus if we're going to win tomorrow."

"Right... right... what were you saying?" Connor asked.

Natalie looked painfully annoyed and responded, "Who do you think should fly with the heavy weaponry?"

"I think Liam should do it. He's scored the highest in the past two targeting drills. I think he's on a hot streak," Connor suggested.

Liam joked, "Why thank you, Lieutenant Blank Brain... I would be honored to carry the pay load."

Connor continued, "We won't know what we're up against but I think Liam should fly behind you and I'll fly behind him. That should cover him from the visible crafts. I think if we trust our instincts in the air we'll be fine."

The next day, Connor found himself in aviation class.

"Alpha Air reporting," Connor spoke into his headset.

"Bravo Air reporting," Natalie sounded off.

"Charlie Air reporting in with a large amount of hellfire and nightmares," Liam reported.

"Stay focused Mr. Hudson," the Captain's voice came into their cockpits. "Your mission will be to escort your heavy fighter over a centralized location within a heavily defended area. The objective is to destroy the enemy Comm tower. A direct hit to the base of the structure will result in a collapse of the infrastructure and ultimately a successful assignment."

The squad flew over snowcapped mountains and a layer of clouds. The steel frames of their crafts reflected the pink setting sun as they headed for the enemy base. Natalie was flying steadily in front of the other two, "No signals yet."

Connor descended to get a better view of the terrain.

"Don't fly too low, Alpha Air. I don't want to be alone when it gets hairy," Liam reported. Connor saw a compound in the distance and ascended back up. He maintained speed closely behind Liam's air craft.

"They're picking up our signal," Natalie reported as laser projectiles started flying all around her aircraft. "Bravo Air reporting... I'm descending to scan for an opening." She flew fast and low around the base clock wise while spinning to avoid their defenses. "Maintain altitude until I get a reading," she said as she zigged and zagged.

Liam's voice came through, "Bravo Air, I'm picking up two enemy aircrafts coming in on your six."

"I see an opening on the northeast side of the base. You should be able to fly over with minimal amounts of resistance, Charlie Air," Natalie said as she made a quick angle of attack and began her turn.

Connor commanded, "Get out of there, Bravo," Natalie's craft began to take projectile fire from the two incoming enemies. "Fly high and head towards the opening, Charlie Air."

"Roger that Alpha Air."

"Bravo. Fly southwest and head for the other side of that mountain peak. Maintain altitude," Connor commanded again.

"Copy that, Alpha Air."

Natalie maintained altitude and pushed the throttle to its limit. The enemies continued to descend and gain speed. "They have a lock on me, Alpha Air. Where are you?" Natalie shouted as her console alarmed her of an incoming impact. She looked at her console and saw a missile rapidly approaching her.

"Avoid impact the best you can and maintain course, Bravo Air," Connor demanded.

Natalie dipped even lower as snowy tree tops waved from the force of her aircraft floating above. She deployed her only set of counter measures and the missile that was tailing her was deflected. "That was too close, Alpha Air," she said with worry in her voice.

She started to round the mountain with the enemy fighters dangerously close behind her.

Connor dipped his craft down right beneath the clouds as the enemy aircrafts were flying underneath. He began to fire on the closest foe. The craft avoided his fire the best it could and moved closer to the side of the mountain. Connor kept firing not allowing the craft to move away from the mountain. He locked on and fired a missile. The missile started tailing the enemy jet, but the pilot released its counter measures. As Connor predicted, the missile impacted on the side of the mountain near the jet causing it to lose a bit of control. Connor fired on its engines and disabled the first aircraft.

A capsule unhatched and a yellow robed operator stepped out and took a seat in anger.

"Very good, Alpha Air! Now make short work of the other," Natalie said. As soon as she stopped transmission, her console alerted her of an incoming missile in front of her. She tried to veer right, but there wasn't enough time. Natalie got up from her capsule and took a seat.

Connor looked ahead as he noticed a black triangular craft fly overhead and quickly past him. "Dominic," he said under his breath. He was still tailing the other aircraft as it led him back towards the base.

"Alpha Air, I have a feeling I'm going to need some back up soon. I'm two minutes from the drop," Liam reported.

"Fly High, Charlie," Connor commanded.

Conner noticed the aircraft in front of him making a wide turn in an attempt to gain the advantage. Connor recognized the movements of the enemy fighter and performed a quick snap roll. He pulled back on the control stick forcing his aircraft's nose up causing him to stall a bit. He then turned his craft back downward and found himself behind the enemy jet again. This time he was closer. He focused on the craft and fired his primary weapons. Lasers shot out of his jet and the enemy's craft separated from its left wing. The craft spun out of control and exploded inside the base. Another student rose from the capsule and sat down in the spherical room to watch the rest of the battle.

Liam continued to climb, and Connor was off to find him.

"I'm picking up a signal, but I can't see anything," Liam reported as he turned his head every angle to find the craft.

Suddenly, lasers shot out of an uncloaked jet. A barrage of fire struck his heavy fighter and disabled one of the engines. His capsule shook, and he briefly lost control.

"I'm hit! Alpha! Report in!" Liam shouted.

Connor said calmly, "Start descending, Charlie Air."

Dominic flew close behind and locked onto Liam. Instantly a burst of lasers flew straight into his front window. Dominic was furious as he stomped all the way to his seat.

"Ok, Charlie Air, I'm coming back around. It should be easy from here on out," Connor reported confidently.

Liam spoke in a panic, "Negative, Alpha. I can't steady this hunk- a-junk."

Connor looked out of his window and saw that they were flying on a projected path towards the Comm tower.

"Maintain speed, Charlie Air."

Liam responded, "Copy, I don't think it'll do any good. I'm going to be slightly off course. I'll miss with the payload." A few moments passed, and Liam did his best to maintain his speed. "We're going to miss the target in twenty seconds, Alpha Air."

Suddenly, Connor flew beside Liam's fighter and drifted very close. He matched the speed almost perfectly and ascended a few feet to nudge Liam's left wing.

"That's… that's what I needed, Alpha Air!" Liam reported as he fired the three heavy bombs at the bottom of the Comm tower. The whole room bursts into yelling and applause. Before the Comm station received the blow, Liam's ship had been shot down by ground turrets.

Both capsules opened and they each crawled out proudly.

"Exemplary form Squad G. That was a motivating performance. Squad H you also performed very well. This has been an excellent and helpful session," Captain Brookmeyer commended them. "We can all learn from the dedication that Squad G put into this mission by preparing."

"We did it!" Connor hugged Natalie and Liam.

"Ha-ha. You did it, don't be so modest," Natalie responded.

They enjoyed the victory and headed down to the common rooms to celebrate with the rest of the offensive squads. Connor enjoyed his night, but it wasn't long until

Natalie and Liam noticed him in a trance. He was worried, and they could see it.

The next day Connor found himself thinking deeply about Alexander Pope. *How can Eden kill his parents? There has to be a mistake. What is he trying to do to me? Should I tell General Marks? Why can't the systems scan me?! I knew this was a mistake. I'm not an operator! It can't see me, and that's why!* he thought.

"Mr. Laurel," the Colonel said sternly.

"Sir?" he answered leaving his daze.

"Have a seat before I send you to the Infirmary!" Colonel Albert shouted.

Connor looked confused. He looked around him, and all the other students were sitting on the mat. Connor was the only one standing up. He quickly fell down and tried to pay attention.

"You have all been very consistent this semester. You have taken your time. Some of you lack balance, but that will come as your body and mind continue to develop. Today I want to teach you something my master taught me years ago. It hinges on one simple fact. Your opponent is never more vulnerable than when they feel safe. This is why in a fight you must always look past your attacker. You must maintain a calm mind that can flow into every movement. Teaching yourself to do this goes against your basic nature. Connor, since your mind seems to be missing today, why don't you join me?" The Colonel directed him to the front.

"Ok, Connor, I want you to clear your thoughts. Take a moment to feel your breath, listen to your heartbeat. Now, while being relaxed, attack me." Connor began to relax but thought about lying in Room 22. He delivered a punch. The colonel slapped his hand away with ease. Connor thought of Alexander Page and how frightened he was to meet him. He delivered a low kick, left jab, and spun to backhand the Colonel to the head. The Colonel was swift and unharmed. Connor felt like he was trying to hit the wind.

"Your mind isn't clear. I can see stress in your eyes, mouth, and stance," the colonel said aloud for the whole class to hear. "Clear your mind! You look afraid; you look lost… your mind will betray your body's every move."

Connor kicked low and then high with the same foot, he tried to sweep the Colonel. He missed. He pushed up from the ground to deliver a devastating uppercut. The Colonel grabbed his arm like he was leisurely picking a flower from the ground. Connor's eyes blurred as he felt the force of his punch send him barreling over helplessly. Connor was lying on the mat and out of breath. The Colonel looked calm and as if he had just woken from a rejuvenating nap.

"Become emotionless… relaxed… your opponents will feel safe. That is all for today," the Colonel concluded.

Liam walked over to Connor and picked him up, "I thought you were a bit better than that, friend."

"Yeh… right," Connor replied.

"Let's go to the Recreation room. I think there's a football game going on in a bit," Liam told him.

"No, I don't want to go."

"Ok. Well, we're going to head that way if you change your mind," Liam spoke. Connor watched as Liam and Natalie left the room.

Connor moped out of the room and wiped a drop of sweat from his face. He looked down at his ornament. It read 3:58 pm. He walked into the Rotunda and made his way down to the row of elevators. *Am I going to die?* he thought to himself. He stepped up to an empty elevator and chuckled at himself. He remembered asking the same question to Dr. Finn in his first ride of the hove rover. That's when he thought he was sick and that Eden was a medical facility. For a moment, as he waited for the elevator, he felt that maybe he was sick.

Guardian

Connor peered around and made sure no one was close.

"Recondite," he said softly. The black doors closed and Connor was on the move.

The doors opened in front of him. His eyes found a small round room. The walls were lined with the same structures that stood in the References room. Hardware and electronic walls slightly buzzed and the room felt warm. There was one tiny pearl colored desk in the middle of the room with one onyx shaded chair. Across from the elevator was a large telescope. The telescope's shaft stuck through the wall and was almost as large as the wall itself. Looking through the tiny end of the telescope was a young man wearing red robes standing with his back turned to Connor. He had long, teased flaxen hair that stretched a bit past his shoulders.

"Hey, Connor," Alexander spoke as he turned around. Connor saw a soft face with tired eyes and defined cheekbones. Connor stood there in a defensive stance. "Don't worry, Connor, hardly anyone knows about this place. I used to love it."

"Don't move closer," Connor threatened.

"Ok, I won't; I'm not your enemy, Connor. I'm here to help you, help everyone."

"What are you talking about? Explain yourself," Connor demanded.

"I was a red robe as you see. However, I haven't worn these robes in five years." Alexander showed his wrist to Connor. There was a large scar stretching around his entire wrist and down to his hand. "I was like you, I lived here in peace. I had friends and felt loved. I had a flaw though... I liked to use my Impetus. I would walk through walls finding every room I could. I would visit offices and areas after hours. They gave me warnings. I didn't listen; I suppose I was rebellious. I started following General Marks around when I could. She was very suspicious. She seemed to stay in her office almost exclusively. One day, I hid on the other side of the wall. I peeked through remaining undetected as I watched her pass through a large door behind her desk."

"The one with the triangular display," Connor interrupted.

"Yes, that door. I waited until she passed through. I ran quickly behind and passed through the doorway. She was standing in a large cylinder tube, it was like an elevator and suddenly it rose up towards the rotating structure above. Unfortunately, she saw me as she ascended. I ran back to my bunk as quickly as I could. I knew that I was in trouble."

He continued to explain his story, "She called me to her office. She told me of the dangers that I could cause. She told me that I was putting Eden at risk. I begged her to tell me what was there. She explained that it was a tracking system. She said it was a basic scanner that searched over the earth trying to find those with an Impetus. I didn't believe her. I ran past her and into the room behind. I tried to ascend as she did earlier, the tube wouldn't move. She came through the corridor with a few staff members; even fat Templeton was there. That's when they banished me from Eden. They told me that they would be watching me and my family."

Connor was intrigued by the unbelievable tale. He lingered on every word.

Alexander went on, "I tried to go home and adjust, but I couldn't. I couldn't remain there with common folk, hiding my Impetus, and pretending nothing had ever happened. I went away for a couple of days. I left my parents at home and told them I was going to visit a friend. I spent three days trying to remove my ornament. It haunted me. I tried every vocal command I could come up with. The ornament stayed on. I tried to smash it with a hammer. I tried to cut the band. Nothing would free me from it."

Connor gazed down at his ornament as Alexander continued to talk.

"So I found a sharp knife. I began to edge out my arm so that I could get the ornament away from me. It took hours of agony and determination, but I finally trimmed enough of myself off to slide out of its grip. I bandaged myself the best I could and headed home. I was still a long way from home when I passed by a river. I threw the ornament off of a bridge and it sunk to the bottom."

He paused and seemed exceedingly depressed.

"That's when I came home and found both of my parents dead. They were murdered. I spent the next three years practicing my Impetus. I trained and learned how to avoid detection. I would break into secure buildings, raise an alarm, and then hide without leaving the facility. I would wait until it was safe again before I would escape. Once I felt prepared, I started to formulate a plan to get into Eden. My plan was to find a way to visit when the Coalition leaders came. It proved difficult as their security was advanced and exceptional. I was obsessed. I kept planning to break into Douglas Icarus' mansion and find a way to come with him undetected. However, as luck should have it, one morning I was walking down the street, and a saw an Eden hove rover fly over me. It was a once in a lifetime chance. I ran as fast as I could, and I hid within the car. Once the car landed in the Receptacle, Eden's scans saw me. I ran into the walls and have been hiding ever since."

"Alexander, what do you plan to do? You said yourself you tried to get to the Edifice and you couldn't!" Connor tried to talk sense into him, "You should go home; you're going to get us in trouble."

"Connor, don't you understand? I'm not going home. If they find me, they'll kill me," Alexander said with a serious manner.

"I don't believe you, the staff wouldn't do that," Connor replied.

"Connor, listen to me! Isn't all of this too good to be true?!"

Connor argued, "It's extraordinary, and it's secure. No one could get to us. No one can harm us. They feed us, they clothe us, they teach us."

"Fine…. Go…" Alexander told him with a defeated frown.

Connor took a few steps back towards the elevator.

"Your opponent is never more vulnerable than when they feel safe," Alexander announced.

Connor froze. He realized that Alexander had been listening in on his combative training class. A wave of fear washed over his body. He was reminded of the entire reason he was brought to this place. He was reminded of why Eden and those with Impetus were hidden from the rest of the world. For security.

Connor without turning around asked aloud, "What were you doing the other night? You were in the Rotunda with your hands in the wall. You had on tight white robes."

"Connor. That wasn't me." Alexander shivered.

Connor turned around. He was timid, but Alexander's tired eyes made Connor look courageous in comparison. "We have to find out, Connor. We have to find out what's going on up there." Alexander said as he slightly pointed his finger up.

"What do we do?" Connor asked.

"We have to get one of the two large keycards. It's the only way we can get there. Dr. Finn likes you; I'm sure you could find a way to get close enough and swipe it from him," Alexander suggested.

"I'm not the one who can pass through walls. There's no way I could pull that off," he explained.

"We have to try something… anything," Alexander said.

Connor frantically questioned, "Fine but listen, who did I see? Who was out that night if it wasn't you?!"

Alexander looked down at his feet and blankly stared, "A Preserver."

Suddenly the elevator doors closed behind Connor. Alexander ran near the wall and passed through. Connor could hear the elevator compartment arriving behind him. Alexander stuck his head back through the wall briefly. "Come back here during the Coalition Picnic, and we'll go from there!" Alexander shouted and disappeared into the wall.

Connor heard the doors open behind him.

"Oh, Mr. Laurel! What a surprise!" a voice came from behind.

It was Professor Ozil. "What are you doing up here?"

"Oh, I came up to check out the telescope," Connor suggested.

"Ah, it is fascinating."

"And you sir? Why are you here?" Connor asked bravely.

The professor continued, "Oh, I like to come up here and plan for my classes. It's more peaceful than References. Not many people know about this place, Connor. Don't spread the word too much. It's a great place to get away. We wouldn't want the entire facility hanging about in here, right?"

"Oh, absolutely sir. I won't tell a soul," Connor replied.

Connor stepped closer to the elevator, and Professor Ozil sat down at the desk with a tablet in hand. "You don't have to run off, Connor. I'm fine to share the room."

"Oh, it's fine. I need to be going anyways,Sir. What's a Preserver?" Connor asked.

"Mr. Laurel!!!" Professor Ozil raised his voice.

Connor froze and was ready to run.

"I didn't realize you enjoyed history… I'll be teaching a great class on World History next year. I always spend a couple of weeks on Eden's History as well. Now let's see… I guess you downloaded some Chronicles from References."

"Um, yes sir. Old things, just really get me going," Connor said nervously. "But you didn't answer my question."

"Quite right, Preservers are mythical in most people's opinions. The last report filed of a sighting was probably in 1904 AD… or 92 FC... However you want to say it. Over 200 years ago. The theory is that they're guardians of Eden who only appear when Eden is truly threatened. It's a nice thought. I sort of wish I was a Preserver. They sound so important with their nice white robes," the Professor babbled.

"Gotta go, sir. Reserves!" Connor said loudly as the elevators closed.

The professor didn't get a chance to say goodbye and seemed a bit perplexed.

Closet

Connor arrived in the Reserves and searched for Liam and Natalie. He saw them talking with two other yellow robed operators in one of the common rooms.

"Hey, guys, do you have a minute?" Connor interrupted the conversation.

"Um… yes… I suppose," Natalie replied in a puzzled manner.

"It's about Aviation class. We have to nail down some stuff before next class," Connor explained.

Liam responded, "Ok, well… sure… let's talk aviation then."

Connor led them into his old bunk, and the room was empty. He searched the back of the room. The lavatory and closet were empty. He got into the closet and pulled the other two in by their robes. They were stuffed into the little room and completely confused.

"Connor, I think that discussing aviation somewhere with a little extra room would be easier," Natalie spouted.

"Yeh! What's with you lately? You're squirmier than Philip talking to girls!" Liam added.

"Shh… I just saw Alexander Page," Connor explained.

The two looked at one another and got very quiet.

Liam whispered loudly, "Why are you telling us, you numb nugget? Go tell Natalie's father!"

"Listen, I can't and you can't either," Connor explained.

Connor went on to tell them the entire story. He told them about Alexander showing him the tablet with the video.

"So you're not an operator?! Or… what? What is the keycard that General Marks gave my father?" Natalie asked.

Connor continued to explain the keycard, the meeting with Alexander, Alexander's claims, Preservers, and every other detail in between.

"Great! Just great! General Marks is going to literally cut us up into little pieces and feed us to Mr. Templeton in a not-so-delicious pudding!" Liam shouted.

"Will you be quiet?!" Natalie said as she stamped his foot.

"Ouch, jeezzzz... I'm sorry," Liam exhaled.

Connor continued, "I don't know what's going to happen, but I wanted each of you to know."

"Hey, don't worry, we're here for you. We'll try to figure this out," Liam comforted him.

"When did Alexander say he was going to make his next move?" Natalie asked.

"During the Coalition Picnic, I'm not sure what that is," Connor recalled.

Natalie interjected, "Smart. My dad told me about that. A few leaders of the Coalitions come and have a picnic with the operators. It happens every year. Everyone goes into the Recreation Room and eats. It sounds like fun, really."

"So what do we do until then?" Liam asked.

"We have to find a way to get one of those keycards. We'll have to think it over," Connor said.

Natalie sounded confident, "The picnic is in two weeks, so we should have time to come up with something."

All of their ornaments vibrated, and they were signaled to head to the café for dinner.

A few days passed, and Connor was sitting in Room 22. He went over to his box and opened it up. He sat his mother's night light out and flipped through his manual. He held up his jacket and smiled. He put it on and closed the manual back inside of the box. He placed the nightlight on the box and turned it on. He walked over to the reclined chair and got settled. Connor looked up at the pulsating dim glow like he had a thousand times before and just smiled. He felt warm in his mother's handmade jacket. He drifted into sleep.

He opened his eyes and saw a large moon floating amongst a sea of stars. He felt a cool breeze. He looked down and saw himself wearing his robes and his jacket. He was standing in a field with tall grass. He heard the sound of rustling water and saw a river in front of him. He thought about the river that Alexander talked about. He imagined Alexander tossing his ornament into the water.

Connor sat down on the bank of the river and watched the dark water slither in front of him. He caught a glimpse of a figure on the other side of the river. The figure was cloaked and hooded. The figure wore dark robes. Connor just stared at him, and he felt on edge. The figure continued to stand there without making the slightest movement. Connor looked at the moon and closed his eyes. He opened them to see the pulsating scanner light of Room 22 shining down on him. He felt restless but closed his eyes and went back to sleep.

The next day, Connor felt exhausted. He went through each class without any attention span. He could only focus on Alexander and the plan to find a keycard. It came time for the mid-day meal, and he walked with Natalie and Liam down to the café. They were sitting down at a celeste colored table and began to eat speckled ribs and bean bread. A digital burly bear growled at Liam's plate. The bear was standing on top of his ornament. Liam flicked his fingers at the bear as the bear tried to slap his fingers as they got close. The bear stood up on its back legs and snorted.

"He's sort of vicious," Liam said. He placed his ornament down by his side, and the bear went away.

Natalie swallowed a piece of bread and spoke, "Have you thought of anything, Connor? I really don't want to try to steal the keycard from my father."

"Yeh right... I suppose you want to rip the lovely Malinda Marks off then," Liam said sarcastically.

"I'm not sure we could do either," Connor uttered, "There has to be a way... I wish we could tell your father."

"That's a laugh... he'd kill us just like Alexander's parents," Liam mumbled.

Natalie stood up tall, "My father is not a murderer!" She said loudly. A few operators stopped eating and looked over at her. She sat back down and regained her composure.

"Of course not, Natalie. No one thinks that. He's only teasing you," Connor said trying to calm her nerves.

"I wish your Impetus was making keycards, who knows... maybe we'll get lucky, and you find yours before the day is over... then you can just waltz up to the Master Room and go in with no problem," Liam halfway joked.

A loud laugh filled the room, and jolly Mr. Templeton marched over.

"Who's ready for the picnic?! I'm thinking of that pacific apple pudding already!!! HAR HAR HAR!!!" Mr. Templeton laughed with an empty tray in his hand. Not even crumbs had survived the day as his tray looked like a wasteland.

"Whelp! I'm off! I have a lot of work to do before the picnic!" Mr. Templeton wailed.

He took a step or two and leaned back in close to Connor. "I almost forgot… I have a... *very special surprise* for you... I'll send it to you when I get a chance," Mr. Templeton said softly. He turned and went on his merry way.

"That was kind of creepy," Liam suggested.

"I agree. I wonder what he's talking about?" Connor asked.

Natalie shrugged and continued to eat. The group finished their meals and left as the table changed into a luminescent tan hue.

Edifice

Connor studied more than usual over the next week. He tried to keep his mind busy. He didn't want to obsess over Alexander and Eden any longer. He thought of every angle, but he couldn't come up with a way to steal a keycard without anyone knowing. He was restless, yet he found solace in reading the textbooks. Connor continued to read alone in the References room. The picnic was tomorrow, and he still had no plan. He thought maybe Alexander had found a way to get a keycard. How would he know if he had? How did he know if Alexander was even still in Eden? Connor was devoured by stress.

He continued to read. His ornament vibrated, and he was directed to Room 22. It was just past curfew. He hiked his way back to the room and sat inside. He stared at the pulsating light. He thought and thought and thought and thought. He thought of scores of scenarios of how he could steal the keycard from Dr. Finn. As he thought, he dropped into a deep sleep.

He cracked open his eyes, and he saw a large moon resting on a dark starless sky. He felt a cool breeze. He was standing in the dark river he had seen before. The water flowed right above his ankles. Connor suddenly remembered the dark cloaked figure. He looked across the river and saw no one. He stepped out of the water and onto the riverbank. He continued to watch the opposite side of the river waiting for the cloaked individual. He heard a soft breath and felt warmth on the back of his neck. He stalled for a moment and turned around. Standing right in front of him was the dark hooded figure. He couldn't see a face. Connor asked, "Who are you?"

The figure didn't answer.

"What do you want?!" Connor asked louder.

The figure started to move. Connor was startled and began to step back. As he did, he began to stumble. Connor watched as the figure reached out to him in the dark. Connor felt the person brush against him as he kept falling. Right before Connor hit the surface of the water, he woke up.

He rubbed his eyes and stared up at the glowing light. His feet felt cold as he leaned up.

He looked at his ornament, and it read 7:30 am. As he looked down toward his ornament, he noticed something past his arm and on the floor. It was a large keycard.

He jumped down, took a few steps towards the wall, and reached down to pick it up. He examined it closely and said, "Alexander! You truly are impressive!" He tucked the keycard under his robes and laid back down to think about their next move.

As a couple of hours passed before everyone in Eden headed for the Recreation Room to enjoy the picnic, Connor felt paranoid as he constantly looked over his shoulder. He walked into the elevator and said, "Recreation."

He entered the room and saw several people walking through nice lush green grass. The roof projected a bright sun and a blue sky. A few tiny, chirping digital birds flew past his face as he stepped forward. He looked over to see that the field had opened up and was now a clear blue lake. Operators everywhere were eating food and sitting at tables and on blankets. He spotted Liam and Natalie speaking with Philip by the water. He made his way over. As he made his way through the crowd, he heard General Marks' voice call out,

"Mr. Laurel, do come here."

He was shaking a bit but managed to keep his cool. He walked over to her. She was standing next to a tall man with silver hair and a smiling, wrinkled face. The man wore strong cologne and spoke with a very proper accent.

"Oh, hello, son. So you're the last brown robed student this year?"

Connor responded, "Yes sir."

"Well, I'm sure it'll come in, I didn't get mine until a little later as I recall. That was many years ago," he joked.

General Marks laughed a little. That was the first time Connor had ever seen her laugh or crack a smile.

"Connor, this is Premier Douglas Icarus."

"Nice to meet you, sir," Connor replied.

"Those good manners will get you far in life. Impetus or not, kindness is a powerful ally." He laughed along.

"Run along," General Marks commanded him.

Connor felt as if he dodged a bullet. He didn't want to waste any more time. Connor ran on and found the other two. Philip had walked over to talk to another group of green and yellow robed operators.

"I have the stuff," Connor said lowly.

"What?!" Liam asked as he laughed. "I'm fine, Natalie may want some though."

"Shut up," Connor fired back.

"Oh! Oh!!!!" Natalie realized. "Liam, you idiot, come on."

They all headed back to the elevators and headed for the Recondite.

Alexander was sitting at the desk with his head down. They entered the room, and he lifted his head. He jumped back towards the wall and frantically questioned, "Who are they? What's going on?"

"They're my friends. They're on our side," Connor explained.

"No! No! It's too dangerous," Alexander beckoned.

"If they don't go, I don't go," Connor demanded.

"Ok, but I'm not responsible for them. I don't think it matters though, how will we get inside?"

Connor held up the large keycard.

"Fantastic! How did you do it? How did you get that?!" Alexander begged to know.

"I thought you left it for me in Room 22," Connor answered.

"No! It wasn't me… It doesn't matter we have to go now. It's our only opportunity," Alexander said as he ran to the elevator.

The four of them jumped inside, and Connor said, "Registration."

The doors opened into the Registration room, and the group scurried over towards the circular railing. As they passed by, Connor looked down and saw the festivities below. They heard the elevator doors open behind them, and a voice cried out.

"Hold it right there!"

They halted for a moment and turned around.

Dominic was standing there.

"I thought I saw you delinquents snooping around. You left the picnic in a hurry, and now I see why. You're aiding a known criminal!" he shouted.

"You don't know what this is about, boy. Go back down to the picnic and forget you saw us!" Alexander ordered him.

"I'm not afraid of you! General Marks will hear about this! General Marks! General Marks!!!" Dominic began to shout as loud as he could.

Natalie looked over at the opening in the middle of the room and was afraid someone would hear down below. She held her hand up in front of her. Suddenly a large piece of adhesive filled and wrapped around Dominic's mouth. He started to struggle and tried to pull the binding strip off of his mouth. Thread began to form around his hands and feet and pulled tightly causing him to fall over.

"You're the best and scariest operator I know," Liam told Natalie with a grin.

"Thanks," she said proudly.

The four of them ran over to the Master Room and scanned the door. It opened, and they went inside. They made their way to the back of the room and Alexander ran through the closed door. Connor held the keycard next to the triangular display, and it flashed.

The door retracted into the ceiling. They walked down a dark hall and joined Alexander waiting in a large tube. Connor, Natalie, and Liam nervously held hands as Connor scanned the card on a triangular display. The tube began to rise and continuously picked up speed. It blasted out of the top of Eden and was flying towards the structure above at an alarming rate. The four of them marveled at the surface below and the atmosphere around them. They could see a horizon on every side of them. Their tube grew dark as it entered into round gap.

They heard a blast of air underneath their feet, and the doors opened to a gloomy room. They stepped in carefully, and lights began to shine above them as they stepped. Their steps clunked on a steel surface as they walked. Their steps echoed through a large corridor. As lights began to shine above them, they saw the structure's roof stretch far above them. On both sides of them was a thick clear glass. They saw large lozenge shaped casings pulsating with veins of white light near the top. There were rows upon rows. They were stacked and lined.

They continued to walk slowly down a corridor.

"Are they batteries? I think they store energy," Liam suggested.

Alexander responded, "It could be, this place is very old and uses a lot of power."

They walked until they came to a set of stairs. The stairs lead them up a level in the same open room. The structure felt like an old cathedral and was full of thick air. They climbed 5 flights of stairs and noticed the room narrowing. They could see the walls clearer through the glass past the rows of capsules.

"I'm not sure this leads anywhere," Natalie whispered. As soon as she finished her statement, she looked ahead to see the end of the walkway. It was a tiny elevator that resembled the elevators they used every day.

"It's narrow. I think only one person can fit," Connor stated as he examined it.

Alexander stepped closer to see for himself, "There's no keycard display, only a button. I think we can fit two at a time."

"Ok," Connor said. "You and I will go first. Liam and Natalie, you two come up when the elevator gets back down."

"Connor, be careful," Natalie said as she gave him a hug.

Alexander and Connor squeezed into the lift and pressed the dimly lit button.

The lift jolted and started to climb slowly. Alexander and Connor stood body to body in the shadowy tube. Connor felt cramped and warm. It was very uncomfortable. A few moments passed and a door opened on the opposite side. Connor wasn't expecting it. They each stumbled onto the ground in front of the opening. They stood up and caught a view of a short hallway. The corridor was gray with hidden glowing particle of lights in the walls.

Before them stood a clear door. It was shaped like a triangle. They walked closer to it to try to see what was on the other side. They saw past the clear door to see a triangular white room. The walls and floor were completely white and were shining brightly. The roof met with a singular point connecting the four slanted walls. In front of them sat white round alloy rings that stacked on top of one another. Connor looked at his ornament. The rings resembled the device Connor was wearing on his wrist. Hovering above it was a deep black sphere the size of a boulder. Behind it stood two openings rounded at the top.

"Welcome, Dr. Finn," a low pitched droning voice bounced off the walls.

As it spoke, the black orb started to shift its shape. Connor thought he was looking at a floating ball of tar or liquid metal.

The clear thick door opened from the middle and as each side slid into the wall. Alexander and Connor stepped into the room. Connor was in awe of the sight.

The black sphere had transformed into a completely black shape of a human without a face.

"Oh… I see. You're not Dr. Finn. Very interesting," the shape bellowed.

"You are the one I cannot see. You have clearance. This is puzzling, but then again, you have caused many errors in my system."

"What are you? Are you a man?" Connor asked.

"I am the Edifice. I am a multifunctional artificial intelligence built to carry out all directives related to humans with Impetus."

"Why can't you see me?! What does that mean?" Connor inquired.

"Your body is like a blind spot in my programming. I have formulated millions lines of codes and protocols to solve this issue. I have not yet solved the equation. In turn, you are directed to sleep in Room 22 in the Analysis Hall," said the figure as its form rippled.

"Why did you kill my parents?! What is your goal?!" Alexander shouted.

"Your access to my information is denied, Alexander Page. You do not have clearance. Furthermore, you are fugitive who has threatened this facility. You will be escorted to a secure location, and a sentence will be carried out."

Alexander screamed at the dark black liquid, "Go Spit!"

Natalie and Liam came running behind them through the open triangular doorway.

They each heard rattling in the openings behind the faceless figure.

"What is your directive? What are you trying to accomplish?!" Connor asked the entity in a loud voice.

"We should go," Natalie proposed in a serious tone.

"My orders are to regulate the amount of Impetus present on the planet. I am to protect them and control this facility so that they may live as my maker has commanded," the shape droned.

"This is impossible…" the faceless black figure said as it began to swell and grow in size.

"There has been a clearance error!" it continued.

Clog. Clog. Clog. Clack.

"The clearance system has been compromised!"

Clog. Clog. Clack. Clack.

"Reprimand them!!!" The dark liquid man bellowed causing the room to shake.

The clear door shut behind them closing them in.

Connor, Alexander, Liam, and Natalie took a step back to catch their balance.

From the openings behind the A.I. device walked out five men moving quickly towards the group. Each man was identical. They wore white robes and black boots; their skin had a slight glow that resembled the shimmer of the light in Room 22. They had black eyes and short hair. Their faces seemed horrific because they were missing a mouth and nose.

Natalie screamed as the men sprinted towards them. One of them came close and punched Alexander into the air slamming him against the clear door. Natalie held her hand in front of her as a rope began to form around one man's foot. The man lifted his other foot and kicked her making her body slide weightlessly into the back wall near the clear door.

Connor began to panic. Liam stood in a defensive stance as one man delivered a blow towards his torso. Liam dodged and pushed his hand away. The second man gave Liam a quick blow to the head stunning him for a moment. Liam spun around quickly and intercepted an incoming kick from the man he had dodged. Liam held the man's leg in his hand and started to shout, "Aaaaaaaaaaaargggghhhhhhh!"

The man's leg began to turn black and burn to its core. The man's leg fell off to reveal a shiny metal make up.

"It's a Robot!" Liam shouted. Connor was stunned by the robotic man's leg falling off. The man's skin stopped glowing and its eyes shut.

Liam was then pushed down and kicked. The force from the kick slid him into Alexander who was still lying on the floor.

Connor slowly took a step back as four robotic men came running towards him.

"We have to get out of here!" Alexander cried out. He latched on to one of Natalie's legs and one of Liam's arms and he leaned back pulling them through the clear door.

Connor stood still like a statue.

"Connor! Run!" Natalie's muffled scream sounded through the door.

A wave of pain came over Connor's body. He felt pressure in multiple areas of his torso and head. There was a burning sensation radiating from his knee.

"NNOOOOOOOOOOOOOO!!!!!!" Liam's voice came trickling into Connor's ear.

Connor's eyes closed, his mind went blank. Dark.... Dark.... Darker......

In the darkness, a subtle voice entered.

"Always be brave, trust your instincts when it matters most," Timothy's voice whispered.

"Discipline... Knowledge... Control... Balance... are your defenses..." Colonel Albert's voice echoed.

Dr. Finn's voice entered lowly, "Sometimes, it just takes a moment... a moment of clarity... to realize your Impetus."

Connor opened his eyes holding his hand in front of him. It suddenly became clear to him. He began to have quick flashbacks. He remembered the sting on his foot during the football game before he kicked the ball with all of his might. He remembered the back ache before falling down in Dr. Finn's office on his birthday. He remembered the headache before the box fell on his head in his closet. He remembered the heat on his skin before he took a warm shower. He remembered the sting on the bottom of his foot before he stepped on the glass.

I can feel it... I can feel it before it happens... he thought in a moment of silence.

The men running towards him seemed to move much slower than before.

With a calm look on his face, he began to fight. The first man attempted to deliver a blow to Connor's head. Connor dodged and kicked the man into the one behind him causing them to fall. Another robotic man jumped and came towards Connor with a right kick. Connor stepped aside and pushed the man's leg into the air and grasping it tightly, Connor spun the man to the ground, and while still holding his leg he drove his fist into its chest. Connor's hand penetrated his chest a few inches, and the man's skin stopped glowing. A kick came toward Connor's head. He lifted his right arm and blocked the impact. Connor stood back up and delivered three quick blows to the robot's torso and spun to deliver a devastating blow to its head. The artificial man's skin went dark.

"What's happening?!" Liam shouted to the others, "How is he doing that?"

"He found it! He found his Impetus!!!" Natalie shouted and jumped into the air.

"Alright Connor," Liam uttered while nodding his head, "Finish the last two."

The last two glowing men came at Connor on each side. He delivered three quick kicks to each of them. They stumbled and came back. Connor blocked a punch on his left. He grabbed one of the men on the arm as he kicked the other to the floor. Connor then struck the standing robot in the face, abdomen, and then knee. The enemy fell prone, and Connor grabbed his head and twisted his neck. Its skin stopped glowing. Connor tried to strike the remaining man to the head, but it dodged. It kicked Connor in the abdomen, and he fell backward.

He was hobbled over on the ground holding his stomach. The glowing man walked towards him. Connor swept its legs from underneath it, and it fell to the floor on its back. Connor quickly stepped over and punched his fist through the artificial man's face. He pulled his hand back. He was holding metal parts that he had grabbed out of the robot's head. The foe slowly rolled over, without light. Connor was moving very, very fast compared to the machines around him. Time seemed to slow or stand still.

"DRIFTER DETECTED!!! ENGAGE AND ELIMINATE!!! DRIFTER DETECTED!!!"

The liquid shadow droned loudly.

Connor grabbed his ears because of the loud sound. He felt intense heat all over his body.

Suddenly a dozen of men came flowing out into the room carrying guns.

Pulsed energy projectiles began to fly towards Connor as he dodged. The black projectiles burned through some of his robes as he continued to move around the room.

"We have to help him!" Natalie shouted.

Alexander bravely ran through the door to try to help Connor.

"Stay back!" Connor shouted back at Alexander. One of the robots directed his gun at Alexander as he got closer to Connor. A projectile hit Alexander in the lower abdomen, and he fell to the ground.

"AAAAGGGGHHHHHHH!!" he screamed in agony.

Liam placed his hands on the clear door. The door began to turn red.

"It's not working!" Natalie exclaimed.

"It won't melt!" Liam shouted as lasers continue to blast in the room.

Alexander began slowly crawling back towards the door.

Natalie fell to her knees and started crying. She held her hands out in front of her. She focused as tears came running down her cheeks. A black handle started to form. From the handle, a curved blade began to extend. The blade was clear. It was made of the same alloy as the transparent door in front of her. Liam was beating on the clear door as he looked back. He was astonished that Natalie had made such a complex object.

"Katana," Liam said under his breath.

Liam knelt down and placed his hand on the blade. The blade began to glow red as he infused it with the heat he produced from his hands. He picked it up and went back to the door. Alexander got close to the door. Liam placed the blade on the ground. Alexander reached through the door and pulled the blade's handle onto his and Connor's side.

He called out, "Connor!" as he slid the blade across the floor. Connor continued to dodge the pulses of energy and rolled onto the ground and took the sword in hand. He began to slice through limbs and guns with intense speed. More men started pouring through the openings behind the dark figure. Connor continued to divide the artificial men with the heated blade. It cut through their bodies as if they were made of water.

The door opened.

"Connor! Come on!" Natalie shouted as she and Liam began to run towards the small lift. Connor veered and curved; he weaved and swerved. He placed a hand on Alexander's shoulder and dragged him past the doorway. Connor looked back to see piles of robot body parts lying in the room. Large metallic bricks began to form and stack upon one another in front of Connor. The bricks rose all the way to the top of the door sealing the Edifice and robotic men in the triangular room.

Connor looked back towards the elevator to see Dr. Finn standing there with Natalie in one arm and his other outstretched.

Connor knelt down to Alexander who was lying in pain.

"Connor, you're the key. You have to find out what it wants," he said as his tired eyes began to dilate. His breathing intensified as Connor held his left hand over his chest.

"Find out why they killed my parents... why they killed me...."

Connor gripped his hand and whispered, "I promise."

Connor closed Alexander's eyes and stood up. Liam, Natalie, and Dr. Finn were standing there perplexed by all that had happened. General Marks arrived in the elevator and ran over to Alexander's body. She placed her hand on his chest, but it was too late.

"Come here, Connor," Dr. Finn reached his arms out.

Connor walked over to him, and they embraced. "You're alright now. We're going to get you out of here," Dr. Finn assured him.

Gift

They went down the elevator two by two and back down the flight of stairs.

"Why did it attack us? Everything was fine for a moment then it came after us," Liam spoke up.

"We're not sure," Dr. Finn responded.

They got into the tube and descended back down to Eden.

"Come on, I'm going to take you all to the Infirmary," Dr. Finn told them.

"I'll find Templeton then I'll meet you down there, Finn," General Marks said as she walked through the Registration Room.

Dr. Finn and the young operators took an elevator to the Rotunda and walked to the Infirmary.

They each sat down in the Infirmary with Dr. Finn. Mechanical arms came down from the ceiling and started to scan them. They all flinched but remained calm.

"You all are incredibly fortunate. Dominic came screaming into the picnic and told us what happened. You can't tie people up, Natalie. I expected more from you," Dr. Finn scolded.

"But, daddy…."

"Enough! And you should have come to me about Alexander, Connor." Dr. Finn told them. "I understand why you trusted him, but now he's dead. What did the Edifice tell you? Why was it defending itself?"

"I'm not sure, sir. I guess it was because I had a faulty keycard." Connor explained as he showed Dr. Finn the keycard.

"Where did you get this?!"

"I found it in my room this morning," Connor told him.

"I suppose that's why the system started attacking you. General Marks and I scanned our cards when we reached the tube in the Master Room," he thought aloud.

"Interesting, this is advanced technology. I'm not sure how anyone could have made this." Dr. Finn discussed as he took out his keycard and held them side by side.

General Marks walked behind Dr. Finn.

"You all could have been killed. As soon as we sort this out we're going to have a very long discussion!" she shouted.

"What's the update?" Dr. Finn asked her.

She explained, "Templeton is working with the system. He thinks he can calm it down or even reboot it."

"Connor, the *very special gift*," Natalie whispered to Connor. He then remembered Mr. Templeton telling him that he was going to give him a gift.

"Alexander was troubled, but he didn't deserve this," General Marks said to Dr. Finn.

"We have to get to the bottom of this," Dr. Finn replied. "I never thought I'd see the day when Preservers showed up."

General Marks assured Dr. Finn, "I didn't even believe they existed. We'll find out why they've come."

General Marks walked over and checked each of the young operators. They seemed to be unharmed. She took out her keycard as she saw Dr. Finn holding the other two. She took one of his keycards and started bending it. It broke in half and grew dim. "There can only be two... I will find out where the third came from! We can't risk operators getting attacked again," she stated. She dropped it on the ground and continued to crush it into hundreds of pieces.

"I'm going to check on Templeton. He better have an answer for this extra keycard if he ever wants to eat again," General Marks remarked as she walked out of the Infirmary and into the Rotunda.

"Dad, can we go to our bunks?" Natalie asked her father.

He responded with a soft smile, "Sure, sweetie. You can run along. You're safe now." Liam and Natalie stood up and headed out of the door.

"Sir," Connor spoke as he continued to stay seated.

"The liquid black man; the Edifice, it said that it couldn't see me. I knew it couldn't see me because Alexander showed me a recording of you and the General discussing it. You made me stay in the scanning room."

"I'm so very sorry, Connor. We only allowed it to continue because it's never happened before. You're special. We were unprepared," Dr. Finn explained.

Dr. Finn asked, "Did it tell you why it couldn't see you?"

"No… it didn't… it told me that it tried and tried, but it was unsuccessful."

"I promise you that we will find out what's going on Connor. No more secrets," Dr. Finn gazed at him. "There is something that I know for sure. You are without a doubt the most powerful operator that Eden has ever seen. I knew your Impetus would show up exactly when it needed to," he smiled and grabbed Connor on the shoulder.

"Thank you, doctor," Connor replied graciously.

Dr. Finn started out of the door when Connor spoke up again. "Dr. Finn, what's a drifter?"

Dr. Finn stood in place for a moment. He turned around and walked back to Connor.

"What did you say?" he asked with a boggled look.

"A drifter sir… the faceless A.I. … it started shouting drifter detected. What did it mean?" Connor explained.

"I'm not entirely sure, Connor. I'll have to research it more. I have heard of that before, if I had to guess, I'd say it meant that it detected a very powerful operator," he said humbly.

Connor accepted his explanation, and Dr. Finn walked out of the Infirmary.

Connor thought about what had happened. He had never been so frightened and never so brave. He closed his eyes and cleared his mind. He thought of home and tried to think peaceful thoughts. As he sat, he caught images of Alexander getting shot. He inhaled heavily and walked out of the Infirmary.

He made his way across the Rotunda through crowds of operators. As he walked through, they began to speak.

"We're with you, Connor."

"We're here if you need us!"

"We're proud of you!"

Voices cried out as he made his way through.

He caught a glimpse of Dominic frowning at him with his arms crossed.

Connor got to Room 22. He walked in slowly and took a seat. He looked up at the ceiling, and the light was dark. It didn't pulsate, it didn't shine, and he felt relief. He noticed that he had left his night light out on the box. It had lost its charge. He walked over and as he picked up the night light, the top of the chest made a wave of light. He opened up the box, and there was cartridge resting on his manual. He lifted the cartridge up, and his ornament began to vibrate.

"Message received."

"Play," Connor spoke.

"HELLO! Connor, I was able to finish up my regular work, and I had time to tinker in my free time. I'm happy to say I finished your *very special surprise*. Just call out your dragon… when it is present say, "Draken." Ms. Finn told me you really love that *Draken* TV show. I'm sure you'll love this. HAHAHA!" Mr. Templeton's voice played.

Connor lifted his ornament up and commanded, "Dragon." The dragon appeared and started to fly. He commanded, "Draken." The dragon suddenly turned into an exact replica of Draken. He waved to Connor and breathed fire ferociously.

Connor smiled and was impressed by the detail of the model. Connor put down his ornament and sat on the reclining chair. He stared up at the dark ceiling, and he had the best sleep he'd had all year.

Robes

The next day, Connor, Liam, and Natalie joined Dr. Finn, Mr. Templeton, Colonel Albert, Professor Ozil, Captain Brookmeyer, and General Marks in the Master Room for a memorial observing Alexander Page's passing. They all agreed to work together to try to make sure that his death was not in vain. They agreed not to keep secrets.

Connor looked at a projection of Alexander. He was standing there smiling and wearing red robes. His eyes didn't look tired.

"I'm sorry, Alexander," Connor said lowly. A hand reached out and grabbed Connor's shoulder.

"You can't blame yourself. He did what he had to do," Captain Brookmeyer said softly.

"But he died, and It was my fault. He never found out what happened to his parents; I just stood there frozen. I could have run; maybe we could have gotten past the wall," Connor tried not to cry.

"Sssshhh! Sometimes when you fight things don't always go your way. When I used to fly for the Coalition, we had kids who got shot out of the air. We always felt responsible. It took me a long time to realize that they carry on. They are fallen angels who continue to watch your back when it really counts. Alexander may not have answered every question he wanted, but you're still here. You can find those answers, and he'll be there. He won't miss a thing," The Captain gave Connor a light squeeze and made his way back over to the others. Connor thought about his promise to Alexander, and he intended to keep it.

The week passed, and Dr. Finn invited Connor to his office. Once Connor arrived, Natalie, Liam, Philip, Zane, and a few others were gathered.

"I'm sure you've been enjoying sleeping in the bunk rooms once again," Dr. Finn commented.

"You have no idea... I did have to adjust back to Liam's awful snoring," Connor responded and poked fun at Liam.

"That's great news, Connor. I invited everyone here today because even though we have had problems in the past week, something amazing and awesome did happen. You received your Impetus," Dr. Finn announced with excitement.

The whole room cheered.

"And in light of that, I present to you, your yellow robes," Dr. Finn said as he walked over to him and offered him fresh new yellow robes. The room continued to cheer him on.

Connor looked down at the yellow robes and smiled. He had spent an entire year wishing for this moment. As he stared at the yellow robes, he thought about how important this was to him.

"What's the matter, Connor?" Dr. Finn asked him. The room fell silent.

Connor explained humbly, "I really appreciate this, sir... but... if it's alright, I'd like to keep my brown robes. I've never felt so alone as I did this year. I don't want any operators to feel like that; you know next year."

"Connor, that is very, very noble. We are all incredibly lucky to have you at Eden. You can continue to wear brown robes if you'd like," Dr. Finn acknowledged.

The thought moved the entire room and they each congratulated him. They continued to converse and celebrate until it was time for dinner. Time passed, and school seemed unimportant. Connor managed to maintain above average grades and was cleared to move up next year. The events with the Edifice made the last few weeks fly by quickly.

Home

The year had ended and Connor had made history. It was time to go back home for the summer. Liam, Natalie, and Connor all said their goodbyes and walked down to the landing bay.

"Hey, Connor. I know you're going to keep wearing brown robes, but I made something extra for you," Natalie told him.

"What's that?" he asked.

She replied, "I put the robes in the back seat of the car."

Connor looked over to the hove rover and nodded.

"Don't start crying when you realize I won't be there to watch you sleep at night," Liam joked as he gave Connor a hug.

Connor smirked, "I think I'll manage."

"Ready?" Colonel Albert asked as he walked to the front of the hove rover.

"Yes, Colonel. Hey, I want to thank you... your training... it saved me," Connor told him as he opened up the back door.

"You have performed above expectations. Your concentration and discipline saved you, Connor. Remember that," he said as he smiled and climbed into the car.

Connor returned home and greeted his parents. They were thrilled to have him home for an extended period of time. Connor felt peaceful at home most of the time, but other times he thought about Alexander. He wondered where the other keycard came from.

Connor sat in his bedroom, and he looked through his grandfather's manual. He felt comfortable with the smell and the feeling of it. He heard shouting through the window, and he stood up to see what was happening. He saw Samantha in her back yard waving.

"Welcome back, Connor! It's good to see you!" she shouted.

"It's good to see you too!" he shouted back. She giggled and ran back into her house.

Connor looked over at the corner of his room. He hung the new model aircraft Dr. Finn gave him when they first met. He gave the mobile a quick push and watched it spin around. He smiled. He noticed his brown robes folded on his bed. "Oh yeh," he muttered to himself as he remembered that Natalie had given him those garbs.

He held the brown robe up as it unrolled towards the floor. There was a small stitched flaxen dragon insignia sewn over the left chest area. He smiled again and realized that he had made the greatest friends anyone could ask for that year.

Connor Laurel paced around his room thinking about the incredible year he had just experienced. Though he still had questions, Connor was finally an operator and perhaps one step closer to becoming a man.

To be continued